Summer of the War

Gloria Whelan

Summer
of the
War

■ HARPERCOLLINS*PUBLISHERS*

www.harperchildrens.com
Library of Congress Cataloging-in-Publication Data
Whelan, Gloria.
Summer of the war / Gloria Whelan. — 1st ed.
    p.   cm.
Summary: Fourteen-year-old Belle resents the presence of her sophisticated cousin on a
family vacation in the summer of 1942, but their strained relationship is overshadowed by the
war in Europe.
ISBN-10: 0-06-008072-8 (trade bdg.) — ISBN-13: 978-0-06-008072-3 (trade bdg.)
ISBN-10: 0-06-008073-6 (lib. bdg.) — ISBN-13: 978-0-06-008073-0 (lib. bdg.)
    [1. Family life—Fiction.   2. Cousins—Fiction.   3. World War—1939–1945—United
States—Fiction.]   I. Title.
PZ7.W5718Su 2006   2005028425
[Fic]—dc22   CIP
                                                                                    AC

❖
Typography by Al Cetta
1 2 3 4 5 6 7 8 9 10
First Edition

For Elizabeth Buzzelli,
whose garden has given pleasure
to so many

Summer of the War

One

In winter's ice and snow we closed our eyes and saw the green island and the blue lake and were comforted. I dreamed about the big wooden cottage painted green so that it disappeared into the trees. I knew every tree and every inch of deserted beach. It made the world better just to think about the summer afternoons that never seemed to end and the long evenings when we sat on the porch watching the sun sink into the lake like a great orange balloon. The minute school was out, we began packing.

This year we were more eager than ever to escape to the island, for in December the Japanese had bombed Pearl Harbor and the United States had declared war on Japan and Germany. The newspapers were full of lists of soldiers who had died and pictures of bombed cities. On the island we seldom saw a newspaper. On the island we would be able to forget about the war.

In past summers Mom and Dad had been with us on the island. Mom would stay all summer keeping an eye on us kids. She would wipe off her nail polish, take off her shoes, and catch up on her reading. Dad would spend a couple of weeks fishing and try not to argue with Grandpa over politics. This year everything was upside down. Dad had talked of going off to war and even started to do push-ups; but at thirty-seven and with four kids, he didn't interest the Army. That was a blow to Dad's ego, but it didn't stop him from wanting to do his part. He took a leave of absence from his position at Ford Motor Company to help supervise the production of B24 Liberators for the Army Air Force. It was a seven-day-a-week, fourteen-hour-a-day job.

Mom was going back to the medical practice she had left when we came along. She was needed because doctors were leaving their practices to join the Army and Navy. She hated to miss summer on the island, but she was excited about practicing medicine again. There were medical journals all over the house. "I've got so much catching up to do," she said. She brought out her white coats, moved the buttons to give herself more room, and modeled them for us. She let us listen to our hearts with her stethoscope and showed us how to make our legs jerk by hitting our knees with her little rubber hammer.

I think if we hadn't had the island to look forward to, we would have felt abandoned with Mom and Dad so wrapped up in their busy new lives; instead we felt sorry for them having to give up their summer vacations. Grandma and Grandpa would be on the island. Grandpa ruled the island. He was like an emperor presiding over a watery kingdom, or he was Shakespeare's Prospero on his uninhabited island and we were the spirits that attended him. Until Carrie came, no one considered disobeying Grandpa. Why would we? We loved him and we loved the island. It was Grandpa who formed our summers. We couldn't imagine a summer without him.

The first week in June, Tommy, Emily, Nancy, and I set off by ourselves for the island. At fourteen I was the oldest and as much in charge as my brother and sisters would let me be. I had two sisters, Emily, twelve, and Nancy, eight, and one brother, Tommy, who was ten. Mom packed chicken sandwiches, potato chips, and carrot sticks. Our suitcases were crammed with summer clothes. Instead of going in Mom's car, as we usually did, this year we would go by bus from Detroit to Mackinaw City, and from there we would take the ferry to St. Ignace. We would be on our own, which made all of us a little nervous, but since we were all together, we were sure nothing bad could happen.

We had followed the same route every summer of our lives, so it was like turning pages in a scrapbook: familiar towns, familiar farmlands, and finally, familiar forests and lakes. If even the smallest thing along the way was different—a new stoplight in one of the small towns, a barn painted green when for years it had been red—we were stunned by the change and couldn't stop chattering about it. Because of Mom's and Dad's new lives, we resented changes and worried that when we got there, something on the island might be different. We wanted everything to stay just the same.

The ferry brought us across the straits to St. Ignace on Michigan's Upper Peninsula. The Upper Peninsula was more wild and more lone than the rest of Michigan. It was like the difference between a wolf and a dog. We scrambled up the stairs to the top of the ferry, where we would have the best view. Lake Huron stretched as far as you could see, and somewhere in the blue distance was the island.

Mr. Norkin was waiting for us with his ancient Chevrolet and four cold soda pops. We had known the Norkins forever. Mr. Norkin caught fish to sell and guided sportfishermen from downstate. He knew the lake so well, Grandpa said you could drop a penny anywhere in Lake Huron and Jim Norkin could find it. Mrs. Norkin sold vegetables from her garden and worked for us one day a week on the island. Since the war began there had been gas rationing, and I handed Mr. Norkin the gas coupons Dad had saved to reimburse him for the trip between St. Ignace and Birch Bay, and then we piled into the car, everyone but Nancy fighting for the front seat.

Mr. Norkin chose Nancy to sit next to him, probably because she was the one who wasn't pushing and scrambling. He collected the empty pop bottles and carefully put them into a paper bag. There was a rumor that he made his own wine with wild grapes, and I guessed it would go into those bottles.

"So you kids made the trip all by yourselves. I heard your ma has gone back to doctoring and your pa's getting bombers built." Since he already knew all the news from Mom's letters to Mrs. Norkin, he didn't wait for us to say anything but launched into his usual complaints. "Worst winter ever." He said it every year. We listened politely to his tales of ice and snow shutting down the small town of Birch Bay and his grousing about gasoline rationing.

"The goverment's allowing fishing boats extra gas coupons, but there isn't enough gas to take sport-fishermen out. Anyhow there aren't any sportfishermen because they don't have enough gas to get up here."

When we reached Birch Bay, Mr. Norkin parked his car in the Norkins' barn, fluttering the chickens and worrying the horses. We got hugged by Mrs. Norkin, who shook her head over how much we had grown like she always did, and then we followed Mr. Norkin to his dock. His runabout would carry us and all our luggage to the island. With an unlit pipe clamped between his teeth and wearing his old, battered captain's cap, Mr. Norkin navigated the channel's tricky current. It was a twenty-minute run across water whose slightly fishy smell made my hand ache for a rod and reel.

"The war's changing everything," Mr. Norkin said. "I'm even hearing some foolish talk from Ned about joining the Navy next spring when he turns eighteen."

I was so shocked to hear about Ned, I very nearly fell out of the boat. Ned was Mr. Norkin's son. Last year he had stopped treating me like a pest and let me go sailing with him. I thought he would look gorgeous in a uniform, but I didn't want him to go off to war.

Tommy was asking, "Are the cormorants back?"

"Yes, and they're ruining the fishing." Mr. Norkin spit to emphasize his disgust.

"Indians use cormorants to catch fish," Tommy said. Tommy knows everything about birds. "They tie something around the bird's long necks so they can't swallow the fish."

"That's cruel," Nancy said. Nancy couldn't bear for anything to be hurt. She stepped around ants and ran away when we slammed the fish we caught against the dock.

"No worse than having to wear a necktie," Mr. Norkin told her.

I was thinking of Ned and watching for the first sight of our island. We passed Circle Island with only a few cottages and then Big Island with its row of summer places and the Lodge, a sort of clubhouse where the island people gathered. Just beyond Big Island was Turtle Island and our cottage, the only cottage on the island. Maybe it was selfish, but I never got over the magic of having an island all to ourselves.

You had to look hard to see the dark-green cottage against the island's trees. It had a big screened porch and a screened sleeping porch on the second floor so you could be inside and out at the same time. A field-stone chimney stuck up on one side of the cottage. Behind the cottage were acres of pine and birch trees, and beyond the trees Lake Huron. In front of the cottage a dock reached out into the channel. Beside the dock was the boathouse where we kept the canoe and Grandpa's boats.

Grandpa had the American flag and the Turtle Island flag flying. As soon as we saw him waiting for us at the end of the dock, we began to wave wildly, nearly upsetting the boat. Grandma was there too, but it was Grandpa we saw, standing there like a proud captain at the prow of his ship. Grandpa was tall with silver hair and eyes that in his tanned face were as blue as a jay's feather.

Grandpa looked like a man in charge of something important, like you imagine owners of ranches or presidents look. Though Grandpa was kind and fair, I always felt intimidated by him, not exactly afraid, but hindered. He never hesitated to tell you when you had done something wrong or give you bad news. He went right at something and just did it. He never changed his mind or gave in on something. If you crossed him, you were in trouble, but in a way Grandpa's firmness was reassuring, because you always knew right where you stood with Grandpa.

Grandma was more easygoing. Before she said something, you could see her thinking about how it would affect you. She liked everyone to be happy. She was the one who smoothed your feathers after Grandpa ruffled them.

It was all I could do to keep from jumping out of the boat and swimming the last few feet to the island. The minute Mr. Norkin moored the runabout, we scrambled onto the dock, throwing our arms around Grandma and Grandpa. We took in our luggage and looked quickly around for any changes. A new jigsaw puzzle lay scattered on the table waiting for rainy afternoons. As usual there were some new books on the shelves, but lots of battered old favorites, too, like *Little Women* and *Great Expectations* left over from when Grandma was a girl. There was the same bright-yellow pile of *National Geographic*, and Grandma had crocheted a new afghan to warm us on cool evenings. After Grandma gave us some of her molasses cookies and lemonade and Grandpa saw that all our things were unpacked and put away neatly in our drawers and closets, we were off to our favorite places on the island.

Emily headed for the flower garden. It wasn't that she liked gardens so much as she liked the idea of gardens. Emily could imagine the ugliest thing into something beautiful. She loved pretty stuff and spent her allowance on things like a handkerchief trimmed with lace. She went around smelling of Mom's perfume and took hours in the bathroom doing her hair.

"Mrs. Norkin's sent the marigolds all ready for me to plant," Emily called out. For some reason no one took care of the garden except Emily, who planted marigolds every year. Grandpa whitewashed stones that set the garden apart and kept it from growing wild, but he never pulled a weed. Grandma didn't tend it either, which was strange, because Grandma was so particular about everything in its place that you could find what you were looking for in the kitchen with your eyes closed. The neglected garden was an island on an island, and only Emily's marigolds, Grandpa's stones, and a patch of trillium that must have been planted long ago kept the bracken and weeds from taking over.

Tommy called, "Hey! The ring-billed gulls are back!" He had the canoe out, paddling to Gull Rock, an enormous boulder sticking up in the lake about fifty feet out from the shore. Tommy was on speaking terms with all the birds on the island. You could hear him sneaking down the stairs at five in the morning to rendezvous with a snit-streaked snook or something equally strange. Whenever we played wishes, Tommy's first wish was always the same. He wanted wings. When he was little, he nearly broke his neck by jumping from a tree, sure that he would be able to fly when he needed to.

Nancy had her arms around Polo, Grandma and Grandpa's ancient German shepherd. "Did you miss me, Polo?" she was crooning in his ear, and Polo was happily licking her face. Nancy loved creatures. When mice overran the cottage, Nancy wouldn't allow snap traps. Instead the mice had to be live-trapped and carried by boat to the mainland, where Nancy explored the nearby woods until she found a place with oaks so the mice would have acorns. When we all sat along the dock fishing, Nancy fished without bait on her hook.

I took off for the south side of the island out of sight of the cottage. The cottage was on the north or channel side, where the water was warmer and calmer. The south side of the island was on Lake Huron. It was the storm side. The water there was cold, the winds strong, the waves high. I wasn't allowed to take the runabout out onto the big lake. I had to keep to the channel. I loved to sit on the storm side on a windy day and watch the whitecaps crash onto the shore. I imagined how, long ago, the French fur traders paddled their canoes past our island, canoes loaded with trade goods in the spring and furs in the fall. The Indians would have come this way too, trusting their birchbark canoes to survive the dangerous waves.

Our island was only one of several along the

northwest coast of Lake Huron. The cottages on the islands, like our cottage, were owned by families from the Midwest, families who had been summering there since the turn of the century, making believe for a whole summer that life was simple and uncomplicated. We had kerosene lamps and a wood stove. Except for the clubhouse, none of the cottages, including ours, had a phone. The islands were like castles with moats all around them. Protected by a ring of water, you believed nothing bad could get to you.

Once a week we put on city clothes and met at the clubhouse on Big Island for dinner with the other island people. The rest of the time our family was totally alone on our island. Grandpa said being alone was a chance to discover ourselves. He said each one of us was an island, and the most exciting discovery we would ever make was to know ourselves.

I thought I knew myself. I was just me who lived half in the real world and half someplace else. I got up and ate three meals and did all the things my family did. The other part of me spent the day with the characters in whatever book I was reading. In my imagination I transformed the island. One day it might be the Greek island of Crete and I would be running through the labyrinth to escape the minotaur. Another time it would be the Galápagos Islands with gooney birds that let me walk right up to them. Although I got along fine with people, something about the lonely and wild side of the island agreed with me.

I liked having some time to myself. Our family was such a close one, you could get a little smothered. Of course, we didn't always agree with one another. Sometimes I quarreled with my brother and sisters, but I couldn't remember hating anyone for more than five minutes. Then our cousin, Carrie, came to stay on the island, and in no time we were pawing the ground and snarling at one another.

It was on our first day on the island that we heard about Carrie coming for the summer. We had all wandered back to the cottage, changed into our shorts, kicked off our shoes, and settled onto the screened porch. At either end of the porch were swings supported by chains from the ceiling. The swings were my favorite place to read on a rainy day. When I was little, the cushions on the swings had bright green and red stripes, but they had faded in the sun and lost their color. In the middle of the porch was a big round table covered with red-checked oilcloth where we had breakfast and played cards.

Our grandparents had built the cottage when my mother and her sister were little. Everything in the cottage had been there forever. Anything that wasn't being used just got put in the attic, where it could be dragged down again if it was needed. At home Mom decorated so that things kept changing. On the island they never changed. The only change to the decoration was a new piece of driftwood or pile of shells.

Grandma poured more lemonade. "How was the trip?" she asked.

"We nearly missed the ferry," Tommy said. "I bet one of these days they'll put a bridge between the upper and lower peninsulas."

"Over my dead body," Grandpa said. "The fewer people tramping around up here, the better." Grandpa cleared his throat and frowned. You could see he had something serious to say and that it wasn't about bridges. He finished his lemonade in a gulp and put the glass down like he never meant to pick up another glass in his life, like he was all finished with glasses. We stopped doing what we were doing, which in most cases was cramming another cookie into our mouths. Nancy, who is easily startled, choked and had to have her back pounded. Grandpa gave her one of his "let's all keep calm" looks.

"I have some news for you," he said. "I had a letter yesterday from your uncle Howard. Caroline is coming to spend the summer with us. She'll be here the end of the month." It was like all Grandpa's announcements: You accepted it. If he said the end of the world was coming, you'd just stop brushing your teeth and doing your homework. If he said it was going to happen, you knew it would.

"Isn't that wonderful news," Grandma said. Half to herself she added, "I'll never know how Howard made up his mind to let her come."

Uncle Howard is Carrie's dad. Carrie's mom, my

aunt Julia, was my mom's sister. Aunt Julia died when Carrie was three years old. Carrie's dad worked for the State Department, and Carrie lived in France with him. In the spring of 1940 Uncle Howard and Carrie had sailed from England to New York on the *Queen Elizabeth*. For the last year Uncle Howard had been working in Washington. I had never met Carrie. For some reason our family didn't get along with her father. It had to do with his taking my aunt Julia to France to live when she wasn't well. There was something else. I once heard Grandpa say, "That man spent more on horses than he did on his wife."

Now Grandpa was telling us, "The State Department is sending Howard to England for a couple of months. It's much too dangerous to take Caroline there. Bombs are falling all over England. British children are being sent over here to get them out of harm's way. Howard knows sending Caroline to us is the sensible thing to do." Grandpa turned to me. "Caroline is fifteen, just a year older than you, Mirabelle."

I haven't mentioned my name before because with a name like that, who would? It's way too fancy for this family and it embarrasses everyone, especially Grandpa, who thinks Mom must have lost her mind. What's worse, it's the name of a plum. "The sweetest and most delicious plum of all," Grandma once said, trying to make me feel better about my name.

The way Grandpa says Mirabelle sounds like he's trying to punish Mom for her foolishness. Dad insisted on naming my sisters and brother himself. The best that people can do with my name is call me Belle, which I hate. In first grade the boys used to chant, "Here comes ding-dong."

Grandpa said, "I expect you to take responsibility for your cousin, Mirabelle, and show her how things work here on the island. I understand she's a smart little thing. . . ." Grandpa sort of stared off into the distance like he does when he's saying something that means a whole lot more than you first thought it did.

I was thrilled by the news. I believed it would be great to have a cousin for a friend all summer. I saw myself showing her around the island, taking her to all my favorite places. I had a million questions for her. I had never been anywhere interesting, and I longed to hear what it was like to actually live in France. I had a good time with my brother and sisters, but I was the oldest. I was always in charge. Grandpa always reminded me that I had to set an example. Someone older could share some of the responsibility. Carrie could be the example for a change.

"I have one more thing to say." Grandpa looked around the porch as if a hungry crocodile might be slithering around. "Caroline will fit into our life on the island. There will be no exceptions made for any—" Here Grandpa paused. "Any eccentricities."

Emily and I exchanged an excited look. Eccentricities! In our ordinary world eccentricities had a delicious sound.

Two

We slipped into our routine as easily as you put on a comfortable old shirt. Dinner around the dining-room table began with Grandpa saying grace. He was a large man, and seeing his massive shoulders and silver hair, you felt God Himself was giving the blessing. I was starved and wanted to grab for the dish of mashed potatoes, with its glob of melting butter, and the spareribs with meat so tender it was falling off the bones, but grabbing wasn't allowed and I had to wait my turn. We all groaned when Grandma carried in the strawberry shortcake almost hidden under a volcano of whipped cream, but we finished every bite.

We were all so full of sun and food, it was hard to stay awake for our recorder session. Each evening Grandma sat down at the piano, Grandpa took up the violin, and the four of us got out our recorders, Nancy with her usual hesitation, for her mind wandered when she played and her fingers often ended up covering the wrong holes. None of us was especially musical, but recorders were simple. We hadn't played since we had left the island last fall, so there were a lot of mistakes, but no one cared—we just laughed and started over. It was magical that the four of us, each one so different, could come together to make the same music. If there had been quarrels during the day, they were all forgotten. When you play music together, you're all going in the same direction. By the end of our half-hour practice we were always as close as a basket of kittens.

After dinner I wandered down to the dock, hoping that Ned would come by with his sailboat to welcome me back to the island. I had known Ned all my life. Even in the middle of winter and a couple of hundred miles away from him, I could close my eyes and picture him just as clearly as if he were beside me. He had dark hair, dark-brown eyes, and high cheekbones. Mrs. Norkin said her dad was a Chippewa Indian and Ned got his looks from him. With Mr. Norkin's help Ned had built a small dinghy that took a sail. Last summer Ned and I had become good friends, and after dinner Ned would sail his dinghy over to the island and take me out. It was a whole different feeling than a motorboat. It was the difference between being a turtle and being a bird.

Ned didn't have any brothers or sisters, so he was fascinated with our family and the way we all got along. He treated me like his kid sister, protective and bossy all at once. Toward the end of last summer there had been times when Ned forgot about my being like a kid sister and confided his frustration in living in a small town where there would be few jobs when he graduated from high school. His parents would never be able to afford to send him away to college. I had things to tell him as well. Things I couldn't tell anyone else: how I worried that much as I loved him, Grandpa would never let us grow up and do what we wanted.

I sat on the end of the dock waiting for Ned, my bare feet dabbling in water still cold from the winter snows. Gulls landed and took off from Gull Rock. There was a haze like a veil over the sun. A school of minnows was curious about my toes. In the distance I saw a sail and was sure it was Ned. Minutes later I was climbing aboard his dinghy.

I couldn't wait to let Ned know about Carrie's coming to the island. I told him, "She's probably super-sophisticated because she's been all over Europe."

Ned shrugged. "Your cousin sounds like she's going to be bored to death on the island."

I just stared at Ned. It had never occurred to me that Carrie or anyone could be bored on the island. There was never enough time for swimming and walking, reading and exploring, or just sitting on the beach looking out at the water and thinking about life.

"Anyhow," Ned said, "I've got my own news. Dad probably told you I'm joining the Navy. I'll be eighteen next May. As soon as school is out, I'm signing up. Maybe I don't know much about destroyers and airplane carriers, but I know plenty about navigation and I can take an engine apart and put it back together."

I didn't want to think about the island without Ned being there. "Maybe you'll change your mind."

"No chance." He must have seen my look of disappointment, because he said, "I'll tell you what—I'll teach you to sail this summer, and when I take off, I'll leave you the dinghy. We'll start right now. You take over the tiller. Just remember it's not like the steering wheel on your granddad's runabout. You have to push the tiller in the opposite direction from where you want to go."

There was no more talk about Carrie or the Navy, just lessons about sailing on the wind, off the wind, and before the wind. It seemed every time I shifted the tiller, Ned was shouting, "No, no, the other way, Belle!" But by the time the sun had slipped into the water and the last gull had landed on Gull Rock, the tiller and I were friends.

One day hurried after another. Time lagged until I looked at the calendar and saw with alarm how many summer days had been used up, just thrown away as if summer were endless. The soles of our feet had toughened, and you could see where we were tan and where our bathing suits kept us white. I knew how to hoist a sail and how to take in a reef. The jack-in-the-pulpits were blooming in the woods. The gulls were making nests, and Tommy had seen the summer's first yellow warbler.

The day Carrie arrived started out like every other, with an early swim in the channel. There was no lolling in bed in the morning, being warm and snug. Grandpa insisted a dip into cold water was good for us. "Wash away the cobwebs," he said. "Get you ready for the day." We tugged on bathing suits still damp from the day before and ran down the path to the lake, hardly noticing the prick of the pine needles and the sharpness of the stones under our feet. The trees and sky had a fresh-laundered look. Screaming and laughing, we jumped into and out of the freezing morning water. In seconds, covered with goose bumps, teeth still chattering, we were in our rooms pulling on shorts and shirts ready to plunge into the day with as much excitement as we had plunged into the channel.

Five minutes later, water from our wet hair dripping down our backs, we were sitting on the screen porch having our usual enormous breakfast of eggs, bacon, pancakes, and hot cocoa. Grandpa, who had a lot of self-control and never filled his plate, finished first. He took a last swallow of his coffee and said, "I want to have a serious talk with you children. Your cousin Caroline should be here in time for supper."

He announced it as if it were brand-new news to us, when we had been talking of nothing else for days.

"Naturally, traveling around most of her life, and with no mother, Caroline has been a little too much on her own, but I'm sure things will work out. Once she's here, we'll soon have her feeling like one of us." I could see Grandpa meant to take her in hand. Carrie would be one more female on the island. I thought Grandpa was getting to be like a rooster in a hen yard.

Grandma said, "I'm sure Carrie won't be any trouble, Everett."

Grandpa gave Grandma the look he gave people who decided to take up his time by saying something that needn't have been said.

I was thrilled to have Carrie. Our lives were so ordinary, I couldn't wait to hear the stories I was sure she could tell us. Though I envied her exotic life, I felt sorry for her. She had no mother, and now her father was off to a country where bombs were dropping out of the sky.

I had a bedroom all to myself that Carrie would share with me. I loved the room. All winter long I kept it in the back of my mind, something to bring out when I needed cheering up, like a piece of candy you hoard against a special hunger. The walls of the room were pale yellow. There were two white metal beds and a chest of drawers with several coats of white paint and a bottom drawer that always stuck. There was a big old white wicker chair with faded blue and yellow cushions. My window looked out on the channel, and the first thing I saw in the morning was the reflection on the ceiling of sunlight dancing on the water.

I was giving up my privacy, which was hard to get in our family, but I was excited at the idea of having my cousin all to myself. To make her feel welcome, I had gathered trillium into a bouquet for our dresser. I had cleared out half the closet, which wasn't hard because I had only one dress, some shorts and shirts, and a few one-piece playsuits that I hated so much I hid them behind the rest of my clothes. I had given Carrie my bed, which was next to the window, so she could look out at the channel. On her side of the little table that stood between our beds I had placed my favorite books: Willa Cather's *My Ántonia*, which I loved because it was so sad, and *Jane Eyre*. I had practically memorized the scene where Mr. Rochester's wife escapes from the attic and creeps into Jane's room with a knife. I couldn't wait for Carrie to read it so we could talk about it.

I think Grandpa was afraid we would waste time by sitting around chattering about our cousin, so he had planned the whole day. There was an hour given over to dragging rocks to help rebuild the cribs that held up the dock. The cribs were square log boxes filled with stones. We had repaired them every year for as long as I could remember. The ground was mostly rocks, so stones were easy to come by.

We had a kind of sled Grandpa had made. We loaded it with the rocks and pulled them to the dock. Every winter the waves and ice wore away the cribs that supported the dock. Every summer we built them up again. It was as if Grandpa were fighting a war with the channel and we were his soldiers. He knew the channel was stronger than he was, but he didn't mean to give in.

Tommy took the job seriously; he took everything seriously. He was skinny, with twiggy arms and legs and enormous brown eyes. He struggled with one mammoth rock after another, calling out each time, "Hey, Grandpa, look at how I can pick this one up." The weight of the rock would nearly buckle him, but you didn't dare offer to help. He was stubborn and independent, which I guess you have to be if you have two older sisters. He took the same interest in the stone cribs that Grandpa did. He would stand on the dock, checking out the way the wake broke against the cribs, an exact imitation of Grandpa. Tommy knew in which crib each one of his rocks would fit. If Grandpa placed them somewhere else, Tommy sneaked back later and put them where he wanted them. Nothing was ever said, but between Grandpa's and Tommy's stubbornness those rocks sometimes got moved back and forth a dozen times.

When we were finished with the cribs, Grandpa set Emily to weeding the garden and I offered to help.

Emily and I were careful to keep Tommy and Nancy out of our way. Tommy pulled up everything he could get his hands on, and Nancy pleaded for the life of every weed. Anyhow Emily and I were eager to discuss Carrie.

"What do you think Grandpa meant by Carrie being 'a little too much on her own'?" Emily asked.

"Carrie lived in France for a lot of years. Maybe the French do things differently." I had had two years of French and I could read it pretty well, but it killed me to have to say it out loud. I hated being called on, because our teacher would throw up her hands in despair and show me how to hold my mouth in a weird way so that the French words would come out like they were supposed to.

"What things?" Emily replanted a marigold that had wandered out of its straight line. She kept everything in straight rows, the plants so many inches apart and the rows so many inches apart like a marching army of flowers.

I pulled up a thistle and yelped when it pricked me. "I don't know." I longed to hear about France. I had read *A Tale of Two Cities* and *Les Misérables*. Carrie must have walked past the Bastille and the square where Sidney Carton was guillotined. She would have seen Notre Dame Cathedral, where Quasimodo had lived.

Emily interrupted my daydreams. "Carrie went to school in Paris. Will she speak English?"

"She's been in Washington since 1940, just over two years."

Emily got rid of an oak seedling, which Nancy, who had wandered back, then picked up and replanted. While Nancy was busy with her seedling, Emily leaned closer to me and said in a half whisper, "I overheard Grandpa tell Grandma that Carrie's father is 'a stubborn, irresponsible ass.' He said Uncle Howard shouldn't have taken our aunt Julia to France when she was sick, and I think he lost some of Aunt Julia's money betting on horses."

"Gambling!" I was shocked. Grandpa wouldn't even let us play cards for pennies. Grandpa was striding toward us, frowning because we were talking and not working. "Lunch is ready," he announced, "and then off to your books." After lunch we weren't exactly on our own, but as long as we read for an hour, we could read what we wanted to and where we wanted to.

I made my way to the storm side of the island. There was a mossy place under some cedars where I was nearly invisible. I couldn't hear anything except the waves slapping against the rocks and, overhead, the gulls complaining to one another. It was peaceful and lonely all at once, the perfect place to read *David Copperfield*. I imagined the island was England and the lake was the sea. I was at the part of the book where Little Emily drowns, and I felt awful not only because it was so sad, but because it scared me that it was my own sister's name. I looked out at the lake and imagined it all happening right before my eyes. With no one around, I could cry all I wanted.

After the hour Grandpa set aside for our reading, we could do what we wanted. If the weather was warm, we went swimming. Sometimes we fished or explored the island for shells or fossils, or we tracked a deer or a raccoon. We had our own games, made up over the years: We were pirates hunting treasure on the island, or Robinson Crusoe abandoned on a desert island, or explorers discovering an island with strange monsters hiding behind each tree. We never ran out of ideas. We were never bored.

I suppose it sounds odd that at fourteen I was perfectly content to be with my younger brother and sisters. That wasn't true back in the city, where I had friends my own age, but on the island it was different. On the island we all seemed to be the same age, as if the island were magic and we were caught up in an enchanted world where nothing ever changed.

Although she was only eight, Nancy usually organized us. It had been Nancy's idea to build a tree house and Nancy's idea to build a raft. That morning she had seen a porcupine.

"Let's find it. Maybe it's shed some quills." The summer before, we had seen Indian quill boxes for sale in Birch Bay, and we wanted to make our own. Reluctantly Nancy shut Polo, who followed her everywhere, on the porch. "So the porcupine won't give him quills," she said.

We didn't see the porcupine, but Nancy discovered a patch of wild strawberries and Emily found bits of lavender and green glass worn smooth by tumbling in the lake. She held them in her hands, smiling as if they were jewels. Tommy collected gull feathers for an Indian headdress. He had a collection of arrowheads and had seen *The Last of the Mohicans* with Randolph Scott about ten times. Next to being able to fly he would have liked to be an Indian. I found an oak tree with low branches making it easy to climb, and we all scrambled up, stretching ourselves out on the branches pretending we were a pride of lazy lions with stomachs full of antelope, except for Nancy, who didn't like the idea of killing an antelope. "My lion found a box of cookies some camper left behind," she said.

It was Emily who stuck a twig in the sand to find the time. "It's four o'clock!" We realized that what we had waited so impatiently for all day was about to happen. We raced back to the cottage and down the path to the dock. Grandma and Grandpa were already there. Grandma examined us. "Heavens! What a mess you all are! What will your cousin think?"

Grandpa frowned but said only, "This isn't Paris. She must take us as she finds us."

The Norkins' boat was making for the dock, but it wasn't Mr. Norkin in the boat. He was probably off fishing. It was Ned. I hastily tucked my shirttail into my shorts and slapped my hair into place—not that Ned would notice.

Ned was an expert with boats. He maneuvered the runabout right next to the dock, and I got my first look at Carrie. The queenly way she sat in the boat suggested Cleopatra in her royal barge with a bunch of slaves rowing her, when it was only Ned at the wheel. There was enough luggage in the boat for a dozen people. Ned threw Grandpa an aft line to secure the boat, and Carrie stepped gingerly out onto our dock and looked around as if she were expecting something else, or something much more.

She was movie-actress pretty, with long blond hair that she wore in a pageboy. She was wearing a pink linen dress with a lace collar, but the most extraordinary thing was her high heels. Anybody knew you didn't wear heels on a boat. Grandpa noticed them right away.

"Good Lord, girl, Jim Norkin would have a fit if he saw you mark up his boat with those heels. Ned, what can you be thinking of?"

Ned blushed. "It's all right."

I could see in a minute that he was smitten by Carrie. She could have started a bonfire in the boat and he would have thrown on the oars to help it along.

It was Grandma who had the strangest reaction. She was staring at Carrie, her mouth a little open, tears running down her cheeks. She pushed Grandpa aside to hug Carrie. "You're so like your mother, Carrie. For a minute I thought it was our Julia." She brushed away the tears. "Everett, that's not the way to greet your grandchild. Pay no attention, Carrie. You'll learn our little ways in good time. Now let me introduce you to your cousins."

We stood in an awkward, ragged line waiting to be named. "This is Tommy and Emily and Nancy, and this is Mirabelle, who will be your special friend. Let's get your things into the cottage, and we'll have a cool drink and you can change that lovely dress for some shorts."

Carrie had stared at each one of us as we were in troduced, and hardest at me. She said in a matter-of-fact voice, "I don't own any shorts. I like dresses."

At this pronouncement Ned's eyes nearly bugged out of his head. He didn't look like he thought what she said was odd; he looked like shorts were the stupidest, ugliest things in the world and anyone who knew anything wouldn't think of wearing them.

Grandpa said, "Well, let's get all that luggage out of the boat before it sinks under the weight. If it's full of impractical dresses like the one you're wearing, we'll get you fixed up with some of Mirabelle's things."

Carrie looked at my faded, grimy shorts and said, "Oh, that won't be necessary."

For the first time I noticed Carrie's eyes were the exact shade of brilliant blue as Grandpa's. There was some sort of electricity between the two of them, as if blue sparks were flying back and forth.

The tug-of-war between them ended as Grandma guided Carrie up to the cottage, with Emily, Nancy, and Tommy trailing along. I hung back to see if Ned had something to say, but he wouldn't look at me. He was helping Grandpa with Carrie's things. I reached for one of the bags. Its luggage tag had the Paris address I remembered seeing on Mom's letters to Carrie's dad: Caroline Westman, 9 rue du Bac, Paris, France. I thought about Carrie's exotic life, feeling as if some book were coming alive right before my eyes. I gave Ned a quick wave, picked up the suitcase, and hurried after Carrie, eager to open the book.

Grandma led Carrie to my room, leaving the two of us together. I stood just inside the bedroom door with Carrie's suitcase. Carrie had piled some boxes on my bed. Even though it was my room, with Carrie there I was a little shy of entering it. I took a deep breath and walked in.

"Is that your stuff?" Carrie asked, pointing to the closet where a grimy blouse and my worn p.j.s were hanging on a hook. I nodded.

"Am I supposed to share the room with you?"

"Yes, but there's a lot of room in the closet, and I've emptied out two drawers for you."

"I've never had to room with anyone," Carrie said.

Not "I've never roomed with anyone," but "I've never *had* to room with anyone."

Carrie continued to look at me. "If there's another room available and this is just a way of making friends with you, I'm sure there will be plenty of opportunities on an island."

I was beginning to be a little irritated. She was acting like I had leprosy or something. "I used to have the room to myself," I said. I wanted to let her know she wasn't the only one making a sacrifice.

Carrie gave me a piercing blue-eyed look. "*Très désolée*, I'm sure. I'll try not to get in your way." She began to drag her things from my bed.

"That's not what I meant," I said. I wanted to walk away, but that seemed rude. Just then Grandpa brought in the rest of the luggage. "Looks like you'll be changing your clothes three times a day, young lady."

After he left, Emily came shyly into the room and settled down cross-legged on my bed.

"Can I watch you unpack all your stuff?" she asked.

Carrie gave her an amused look. "The more the merrier."

I dropped down next to Emily, and we watched Carrie pull out one dress after another.

"Who does the washing and ironing?" Carrie asked, holding up a wrinkled dress.

"We wash and iron our own things," I said. "Well, Nancy and Tommy don't. They're too young, but Emily and I do."

"How quaint," she said.

"I'll do yours for you," Emily volunteered. She was staring at Carrie's ruffled nightie and the piles of underwear with lace on them. "Is that silk?" she asked. "We've never had anything but white cotton underwear." She reached over and touched the silk.

"Of course they're silk. And they have to last me. It's horrible, but with the war you can't get silk anymore." She placed a little pile of pink silk in one of my dresser drawers. Hers were already filled, and now she was pushing my stuff to one side. When she had finished her unpacking, she said, "If you two have something else to do, I'm going to have a *petit somme*."

Emily's eyebrows flew up. "Is that French? What does it mean?"

I was going to say, "A little nap," but Carrie said it first.

Carrie sank down on the bed with her back toward us, her face nuzzled into the pillow. I pushed Emily out ahead of me and closed the door, none too softly. I didn't like being thrown out of my own room.

"I think she was crying," Emily whispered.

"She's just rude." But I wasn't so sure. The island was the most normal place in the world to me, but maybe it seemed strange to Carrie. Or maybe she was worried about her father.

Emily sighed. "She's gorgeous. I wonder if I could make my hair look like that."

"You could if you wore curlers every night.

Personally, I'd rather die."

We tiptoed around so it would be quiet for Carrie. When it got to be six o'clock and time for dinner, Grandpa looked at his watch.

"Mirabelle, go upstairs and tell that child dinner is ready and we're waiting for her."

"She's probably tired from her long trip, Everett," Grandma said.

"Nonsense. I don't believe that girl ever rests. It looks like she's her father's child. She has one of those minds that are always busy on what little advantage they can manage for themselves."

As I hurried upstairs, I heard Grandma's shocked voice. "Everett, that's a terrible thing to say about your own granddaughter!"

Grandpa was always so fair, but he seemed to have taken a dislike to Carrie. I opened the bedroom door, uncertain of what I would find.

Carrie had changed her clothes. She was wearing a cotton dress with a full skirt and puff sleeves. Her shoes were the exact blue of her dress. Each shoe had a little blue leather flower.

"It's time for dinner," I said. I tried to make my voice as friendly as possible. I thought it would be awful to have to share my room with someone I was fighting with.

"Really?" Carrie said. "Dad and I never eat until eight. Seven thirty at the earliest." She swept out of the room, while I tagged along behind her.

Emily practically gasped when she saw the flowers on Carrie's shoes.

Grandpa said grace before dinner like he always did, and added, "We thank you, Lord, for the blessing of Caroline's presence among us, and we welcome the opportunity to have her join our family and to share the beauty of our island. Amen."

Carrie squirmed in her chair. It looked like she thought joining our family was more of a punishment than a blessing.

Grandma had gone all out to make the supper a special one. She had roasted one of the Norkins' chickens, and there was her special dressing with chestnuts, early fresh peas, and for dessert a gorgeous sunshine cake with thick lemon frosting.

"Do you have someone to cook for you and your father?" Grandma asked.

Carrie shrugged. "There's our housekeeper, Louise, but she doesn't really cook. Papa and I mostly eat out." Carrie pronounced papa in the French way with the accent on the last syllable. Carrie added, "There are some very good French restaurants in Washington." Something about her tone suggested French food was a lot better than what we were offering.

Nancy had been watching Carrie. "You hold your fork with your left hand. Are you left-handed?" she asked.

"It's the European way," Carrie said, "keeping

your fork in your left hand after you've used your right to cut your meat."

I noticed Grandpa's eyebrows fly up.

"What's Paris like?" Emily asked. She was making a few clumsy attempts to hold her fork the way Carrie held hers.

"It's the most beautiful city in the world." Carrie's voice was fierce, as if somehow we were the German enemy attacking Paris.

Grandpa smiled. "I agree with you, Caroline. Your grandmother and I spent our wedding trip there."

"We stayed at the Élysée Palace Hotel on the Champs-Élysées," Grandma said. "It had just opened, and it was so elegant. In the afternoons we would sit for hours at a time in the cafés."

Grandpa said, "Well, we did more than sit about in cafés. Paris is certainly the most civilized city in the world."

Carrie smiled gratefully at Grandpa, and we all relaxed.

The truce between Grandpa and Carrie ended after dinner, when Grandpa handed Carrie a long narrow box.

Carrie opened it eagerly, but when she saw a wooden recorder, she looked around at us, disappointed and puzzled.

Grandpa explained, "Your cousins all play the recorder, Caroline."

For the last week we had been working on a

Vivaldi concerto. I loved the skipping, happy sound of the music when we were all playing in harmony. It was the time of day when without any words we were closest.

"You're just beginning," Grandpa told Caroline, "so we'll try a simple piece, and Mirabelle will explain how the recorder works."

Carrie put her recorder back into the box. "I'm not musical," she said.

"Nonsense," Grandpa said. "It's only a matter of practice. We'll soon make a musician out of you. Now, pick up your recorder."

Carrie got up. "I'm going upstairs." She left.

I saw with amazement that Carrie meant to do as she pleased. It was shocking. No one ever disobeyed Grandpa. It wasn't that he would punish us or anything. It was just that he was Grandpa, and his word was law. I felt a delicious shiver, something you might feel at the sight of a volcano going off near you, but not so close you were in any danger. I stole a look at Grandpa. His face was red and his lips were folded into a thin line, but all he said was, "We'll go on with the Vivaldi."

Grandma held her hands over the piano keys, Grandpa gave the signal, and we began. There were more mistakes than usual. We all felt Carrie's absence. Somehow she had taken the joy out of our playing, making it unimportant and even stupid. When Nancy had played the wrong note three times in a row, she put down her recorder.

"I'm just not musical," she said, and fled outside.

It was one thing for Carrie to decline to play, but Nancy's refusal was revolution. Grandpa squared his shoulders and told us to continue.

When Grandpa dismissed us, I went outside looking for Nancy. I wanted to tell her she couldn't just run away like that, but I couldn't find her. I guess I didn't try too hard. I didn't see why I had to be the one to watch over my sisters and brother. I began to think it was unfair for Mom and Dad not to be there.

Though it was early evening, the sun was still shining. All that brightness got in the way of my unhappiness. I walked down to the water, kicking the sand as I went. A hundred yards off the island I saw Ned's sailboat skimming the lake. I waved, and he put the boat about and made for the dock.

"You by yourself?" he asked.

Though he hadn't exactly said so, I guessed he was asking where Carrie was. He had probably been tacking back and forth hoping she'd appear. More crossly than I intended, I said, "Carrie's upstairs."

He gave me a sidewise glance. "What's the matter? You look like you could wrestle a wildcat. If you promise not to scuttle the boat, I'll give you a sail. Get in. You need a little practice with coming about."

Ashamed of my surliness and anxious to escape, I climbed eagerly into Ned's boat. "Thanks."

"What makes you so ornery?"

I wanted to say something about Carrie, but I didn't think it was right to complain about family. "Nothing. Can I take the tiller?" He made room for me in the stern. There wasn't a ripple on the lake. The pale blue of the water and the blue sky melted into each other at the horizon. It was hard to tell whether we were sailing on the water or in the sky. Even the gulls, gliding above us, were silent. Ned adjusted the sails, working to capture whatever air he could.

My anger with Carrie disappeared. She would be there for only one summer. There had been summers without her and there would be summers after her. What harm could she do in one summer? I was there in Ned's boat on a perfect June evening with Ned only inches from me. I could have reached out and touched Ned's arm.

The last wisp of breeze disappeared. The sails luffed and the telltale at the top of the mast drooped. We were becalmed, but I didn't care. I could have floated there forever.

"How long is your cousin going to stay?" Ned asked.

"All summer."

"Maybe she'd like to go sailing with us sometime."

"Sure." So there was Carrie again. Ned would have liked to have her with him instead of me.

Ned, puzzled by my silence, tried the war. "Eisenhower is on his way to London. Isn't your cousin's father there?"

He couldn't keep off the subject. Mad at Carrie, mad at Ned, I said, "Yes, and I wish she was with him."

Ned looked at me. After a few minutes he said, "Guess we aren't going to get enough wind tonight for a lesson. I'll row us in." He picked up the oars and sculled back to the dock. I was furious with Carrie and with Ned, but most of all with myself. I felt as if I had no control over what I said, as if loathsome, ugly words were waiting inside me like snakes and toads looking for a chance to sneak out before I could stop them. I hopped onto the dock, hurrying so Ned couldn't see my tears. "Good night," I said over my shoulder.

He didn't bother to answer.

Nancy and Tommy were sitting at the porch table playing go fish, Polo asleep on Nancy's feet.

"You want to play?" Nancy asked.

I shook my head.

In the living room Grandpa and Grandma were listening to the war news on the radio. "Finally some good news from the Pacific," Grandpa said. "We've launched an offensive in the Midway Islands." I made some sort of sound to indicate that was good news, though I had no idea where the Midway Islands were. I hurried up the stairs not wanting to think that there were islands where people were fighting one another, not wanting to think about war at all and especially not here on our island.

Three

When I walked into my room, I found Carrie putting Emily's hair up, taking pains to get each curler right.

"I'm going to have a pageboy tomorrow." Emily sighed. "Only I wish I had blond hair like Carrie does." She pointed to the closet. "Carrie let me iron some of her dresses."

"I'm sure that was really generous of her." I tried to keep the sarcasm out of my voice.

I noticed that the books I had placed on the night-stand had been pushed aside. In their place was a pile of fashion and movie magazines.

"Carrie's telling me the plot of *Rebecca*," Emily said. Emily loved movies. She really believed everything she saw up on the screen. Before we went to see a movie, Mom always asked, "Are you sure you have enough handkerchiefs, dear?" Emily cried over everything.

"*Rebecca* is my favorite movie." Carrie reached into one of her suitcases and pulled out a photograph of Laurence Olivier, who had starred in the movie. "Dad got me this picture with Olivier's autograph on a trip he took to England."

Emily was awestruck. "Olivier is gorgeous. Tell us the rest of the plot, Carrie. Mom and Dad wouldn't let us see the picture. They said it wasn't suitable for kids."

"Well, it turns out his wife wanted him to kill her. Then when they got back to Manderlay, the house was on fire." Carrie went on to describe the fire. She made it so real, she might have actually been there. I thought she was as believable as any actress. It scared me to think you would never be sure if it was Carrie or a part she was playing.

Grandma came in to collect Emily and to kiss me good night. She kissed Carrie, too. "It was so nice of you to take time with Emily. We're very glad to have you here, dear," she said. Grandma ushered Emily out the door.

Carrie asked, "Is there a town around here with stores and a movie theater?" She made it sound like someone dying of thirst in a desert asking if there was a waterhole nearby.

I took a grim pleasure in telling her. "There's a grocery and a hardware and a boat shop on the mainland," I said, "but not the kind of stores you mean. The nearest movie theater is miles and miles away."

Carrie looked shocked. "What do you do all summer?"

"Swim, explore the island, read a lot, play cards."
I couldn't resist. "Practice the recorder."

"I might just as well be in prison. Aren't there any boys?"

"There are some boys on the other islands. We see them at the Lodge when we go there for dinner."

"What about that boy who brought me over?"

"Ned?" I kept my voice light. "He's around."

Carrie took a lot of bottles and lotions with her to the bathroom. I was in bed when she returned, her hair in curlers and wearing a pair of white cotton gloves. When she saw me staring, she said, "I've got this fabulous French cream that keeps my hands soft."

She picked up one of her magazines to read, and I read another chapter of *David Copperfield*. I couldn't concentrate. I kept wondering what Carrie's life had been like. I asked, "Who stayed with you while your father was gone all day?"

"Louise. I could twist her around my little finger."

"I can't twist my grandparents around my little finger, and you won't be able to either."

"Why is our grandfather such a bear?"

"He isn't," I said. "He just likes things done a certain way."

"His way," Carrie said. "Well, he's not going to tell me what to do." She flung her pillow on the floor. "Pillows give you a double chin."

It was after our lights were out that Carrie asked,

"Do you miss your parents?"

"Yes," I answered. I did. I missed the way Dad liked to show me how things worked. Last summer he had let me drive on the back roads near Birch Bay. He had even taught me how to change a tire.

"If you're going to drive, you need to know how to handle a car in an emergency," he said.

I saw things on my walks with Dad that I never noticed on my own, like the scrapes on boulders made by glaciers millions of years ago. He made me feel that anything could be explained if you thought hard enough about it.

I missed Mom just as much. I was proud that she had been one of only two women in her medical school class. Though she didn't practice after we came along, she always said she was on full-time duty at home, painting skinned knees with iodine and giving us chest rubs when we had colds. "The best thing when you're sick," she said, "is a big dose of TLC, tender loving care." That's what she gave us. Although I hated myself for it, I couldn't help but resent the fact that she was now giving all that TLC to other people.

So when Carrie asked if I missed my parents, I said I did. "Do you miss your father?" I asked Carrie.

In the moonlight I could see her suddenly sit up in bed and look over at me. "I miss *both* my parents," she said.

I felt stupid and started to apologize. "I didn't

mean . . ." I began, and didn't know where to go after that, but Carrie just flopped down in bed and turned on her side away from me.

I lay awake thinking about the day, going over everything that had happened. Grandpa said it was foolish to try to dig everything up and do it over. I couldn't help myself. I don't think I ever believed our island was a paradise, but it was close. We lived in a small world of our own making, like a kindergarten drawing with a big sun and friendly beasts and everyone in the drawing with wide smiles on their faces. Part of the island's pleasure was the way it let us escape from our everyday life in the city, from snow and school and worrying about what to wear and how your friends felt about you.

On the island there was no one to worry about except ourselves. Often we didn't even see a newspaper, so the war was no more than announcements on the radio. I had thought Carrie would come and just be like us. I never imagined she might not want to be a part of our life on the island. I thought the island was perfect. I never dreamed that Carrie might hate it.

The next morning I tried to get Carrie up to go for our early-morning dip.

"Go away. It's the middle of the night!"

"It's eight o'clock. We do it every morning. It's not bad once you jump in."

Carrie turned over and opened one eye. "I can't come. I'm *indisposée*."

I stared at her for a few seconds trying to translate the word. "You mean you have the curse?"

"That's a vulgar word," Carrie said. She turned over and closed her eyes.

Downstairs I explained in a whisper to Grandma. Grandpa was looking at the stairway. "Where's Emily?"

Grandma said, "She doesn't want to get her hair wet."

Grandpa ordered, "Mirabelle, tell Emily to get down here."

Emily dragged herself down the stairway, curlers still in her hair. "I'm only going in up to my neck," she announced.

Nancy was giggling at the curlers. Tommy said, "You look like you've got snakes in your hair, like that Greek lady Medusa."

We straggled toward the channel, Polo tagging along behind us. Overhead the gulls shrieked like they did when rain was coming. Clouds covered the sun. The air was so thick with moisture, you could have eaten it with a spoon. Nancy, Tommy, and I jumped off the dock. Emily waded in carefully. A second later Tommy was swimming toward her, kicking as hard as he could.

"Tommy," Emily screamed, "you're splashing me on purpose. Stop it!" She reached out and hit him.

Tommy stood up in the water staring at her, not believing what had happened. Hitting was unthinkable.

Tommy and Emily both broke into tears at the same time. Emily ran for the house. Tommy stomped along behind her. Polo was barking. Nancy grabbed at my hand and hung on. A light drizzle started, the drops warmer on us than the channel water had been.

Carrie was downstairs wearing a blue-flowered sundress, her long blond hair in a perfect pageboy. I ignored her and hurried up the stairs to our room. After I changed out of my bathing suit, I stood for a minute at the window looking out at the rain dimpling the lake and putting a shine on the trunk of the maple tree. Usually I liked the rain. It made the cottage cozy. This morning, after what had happened, the rain was depressing, making me feel shut in. I wouldn't be able to escape Carrie.

The sky darkened, and wisps of fog played hide and seek with the channel. The porch was gray and gloomy, so Grandma set the table in the dining room. Emily, her eyes red, had combed out a straggly pageboy. Tommy kept his chin tucked in and his eyes on his plate. Instead of the usual chatter no one said much more than "pass the butter" and "can I have the syrup," until Carrie, looking out at the rain, asked, "Do you have storms on the island?"

Grandpa said, "Well, we get a couple of good ones each summer."

Carrie echoed, "Good ones?" She looked as if she wished she were a thousand miles away.

Grandma sensed something was wrong and tried

to cheer us up. She hated to see anyone unhappy. She was like a polite hostess, always watching to see that everyone was having a good time. "This is just the kind of day to accomplish something I've been putting off," she said. "I'm thinking about tackling the attic. Who wants to help?"

The attic got cleaned once a summer. Usually we all volunteered. The attic was full of boxes of books and magazines and collections someone had put together of stones and dried flowers. There were trunks of old clothes that Grandma let us try on. It seemed no one had ever thrown anything away. That gave me a good feeling, as if it were possible to hang on forever to all the things you loved. Today the attic just seemed full of ancient junk. The others must have felt the same way, for none of us volunteered.

Grandma tried again to interest us in something, "How about a little card game?"

Grandpa said, "A good idea." He loved cards. The only thing he liked more than winning was having one of us beat him. "What'll it be? Hearts? Five hundred rummy?"

"Can you play poker?" Carrie asked.

"Well, of course I can," Grandpa said, "but your cousins don't know how." After a moment he added, "No reason why they can't learn. Why don't you teach them, Caroline. I'll help you if you don't remember everything."

"Oh, I'll remember." Carrie smiled up at Grandpa.

"My father taught me, and I used to play with Louise all the time. Once I won her whole week's wages."

Grandpa's face reddened. "Well, we don't play card games for money here, just for the pleasure of the game."

Carrie was a quick teacher. We were soon calling out, "Hit me with two cards," or "I'm folding." For the first time since she had arrived, Carrie came alive. She shuffled the cards like a professional and insisted on cutting the deck when someone else dealt.

The game went quickly. Grandma was pleased because everyone seemed to be having a good time. When the game was over, Carrie was the winner. "If we had been playing for money," she said, "I would have cleaned up."

Grandpa laughed. "You certainly know how to slap those cards down, young lady."

We had been playing for two hours and we were all in a good mood. I began to think that if we just met Carrie halfway, the summer would be saved.

I happened to look at Tommy. His face was white and his eyes huge. He threw down his cards and marched out of the room. We all looked surprised.

"Well," Grandpa said, "I've never known Tommy to be a sore loser. Just let him sulk."

Emily and Nancy went to set the table for lunch, Polo, hoping for something from the kitchen, at their heels. Carrie settled beside Grandpa, who was getting the news on the radio. I followed Tommy upstairs. I didn't believe for a minute he was a sore loser. I thought he was still unhappy about his quarrel with Emily. I wanted to tell him to forget what had happened that morning. He was huddled on his bed, his arms around his teddy bear, which he dropped as soon as he saw me, embarrassed to be caught with it.

"Go away." His lower lip was sticking out like it did when he was upset.

"Hey, it's me. I know Emily is really sorry about what she did. She feels miserable."

"It's not about that."

"Then what?"

Tommy gave me a long look. "She cheated."

"Emily?"

"Carrie."

"How do you know?"

"I was sitting next to her," Tommy said. "I saw. She took cards from the bottom of the deck."

"Why didn't you say something?"

"What was I supposed to say? 'I saw you cheat'?"

"That's exactly what you ought to have said. I'm going to talk to her."

He shrugged.

I waited until after lunch, when Carrie was alone. She had gone up to our room and was sitting on her bed putting on nail polish.

I came in and closed the door behind me. "Tommy says he saw you deal cards from the bottom of the deck."

Carrie waved her hand to dry the polish. "No big deal." She grinned. "No pun intended."

"It is a big deal. We don't cheat here."

"I know. You're all perfect, the perfect family. Then I turn up like a rotten apple."

"What do you mean?"

"I mean you think I'm some kind of leper because I don't want to jump into the ice-cold water before it's even daylight or play that stupid recorder or read all those boring books you piled up next to my bed. And it's not just me. I know Grandpa doesn't like my dad. I overheard Dad say that your family blames him because he took my mother to France when she was sick. Well, Dad said she wanted to go and the doctors there took good care of her. Now I'm locked up on this island like a prisoner for weeks, and you all think I'm some sort of idiot. So what if I cheated at cards? It just proves you're all not as smart as you pretend to be. Papa says people are just waiting to be fooled."

I had come barging into the room eager to accuse Carrie, and all the time she was thinking we hated her. "Look, you're all wrong about us," I said. "We don't think we're perfect. It's just that we've always done things a certain way, and I guess we thought you'd want to do them that way, too."

"You're not interested in what I like or what I want to do. It's your way or nothing. Anyhow, I don't belong here. I should be with my papa. I'd rather have bombs dropping on me than everybody trying to make me into one of you."

"I'm sorry if we made you feel like an outsider. When you get to know us, you'll see we're all different."

She was blinking her eyes to keep back tears. "Are you going to tell Grandpa I cheated?"

I shook my head. "You won't cheat again?"

She wiped away the tears with the back of her hand and grinned at me. "I don't have to. I can beat all of you without cheating."

Four

The next morning Emily positively refused to go in the water. "Where everyone is splashing around," she said, giving Tommy a sharp look.

When Grandpa called us to help him build up the cribs, Carrie said, "Moving stones around is the kind of work prisoners do. This might as well be Alcatraz Island. Besides, it would ruin my nails."

"So what are we supposed to do," Tommy asked, "let the lake wash away the whole island?"

Under her breath so that only Tommy and I heard her, Carrie said, "That would be fine with me."

Tommy gave her an angry look. He hadn't forgiven her cheating. I had promised him that she wouldn't do it again, but he didn't believe me.

In the past I had enjoyed the half hour we spent filling in the cribs, bragging about the size of the stones we were lifting, finding the stone that fit a certain place, winning the battle with the water and the currents. Just seeing Grandpa's pleasure in what we accomplished made it fun. With Carrie standing there watching us, a superior look on her face, I did feel like a prisoner on Alcatraz. Carrie had spoiled all the pleasure. Grandpa and Tommy were the only ones who worked as hard as usual. If Grandpa noticed how little we were doing, he didn't say anything.

Since talking with Carrie, I kept seeing us not the way we had always been, but as Carrie saw us. I honestly wanted to be friends with her. I think I even hoped that in the weeks she was with us, some of her sophistication would rub off onto me. Once I had held a butterfly lightly, and when I let it go, a little of the bright dust of its wings remained on my hands. I hoped that if I could just learn a little of Carrie's sophistication, Ned might look at me like he looked at Carrie.

I tried to think of something that would please her. Grandma had given me the weekly list of groceries to get on the mainland. Now I asked, "You want to come with me?"

She headed for the closet. "Never mind changing your clothes," I said. "It's only Birch Bay. And don't wear heels on the boat." Grandpa had two boats, the runabout and his Chris-Craft. He was fanatic about both of them, keeping their wood lacquered like fine pieces of furniture and their brightwork polished to a gleaming shine. The proudest day of my life was when Grandpa allowed me to take the runabout out on my own. That was only after I had crossed the channel a million times under his watchful eye, memorizing all the shoals and boulders that lay just beneath the surface of the water ready to tear open the boat's hull.

Carrie didn't wear heels, but she did change her clothes, and I wondered what the people in Birch Bay would think of a girl who dressed as if Birch Bay were New York City and she were going for a stroll on Fifth Avenue. She was wearing a white eyelet blouse and pleated pink skirt.

It was Mrs. Norkin's day to help Grandma with the cooking and cleaning. As we left, Mrs. Norkin called out, "See that Ned doesn't give you any green potatoes, Belle, and bring back some rhubarb. I'll make a pie."

Birch Bay was a fishing town. The boats went out each morning and came back with a load of whitefish and perch thrashing about on the bottom of the boat. The fish were cleaned and iced and sent all over the state. The town had a large hotel for summer people, but once the war started, the big steamers no longer brought people up the lakes from Detroit and Chicago, so the hotel had closed.

On the outskirts of the town there were a few small farms, but the sandy soil and the long winters kept anyone from making much of a living farming. The main business, apart from logging, was taking care of people like us who summered on the islands.

Along with the post office, the boat repair shop, the hardware store, and a small grocery, there were carpenters and a plumber and electrician. I loved the town. On a summer's day there was a slowness to everything you never found in a city. You said hello to anyone you met because you knew them and they knew you or about you.

Carrie must have seen the town when she came to the island, so I thought she would know what to expect, but she kept looking behind the small string of buildings on the main street as if they were just a stage set for some movie, and lurking behind them must be a real town.

"What do these people do?" she kept asking, as if it were impossible for human beings to live normal lives in a town like Birch Bay.

Until gas rationing there had been a mailboat that delivered letters to the islands. Now our first stop was the post office. Mrs. Newcomb handed me two letters, both from Mom and Dad, one for us kids and one for our grandparents. Mrs. Newcomb smiled at Carrie. "You must be Caroline Westman. I have a letter for you, too. It looks like it's from your father all the way from England." The letter was on thin blue airmail stationery with the face of a king on the stamp. I thought of the distance the letter had traveled and the strangers who had handled it and how far away Carrie's father was.

Caroline gave Mrs. Newcomb a cold look, as if she

were angry that the postmistress knew all about her. As soon as we were outside, she tore open the letter, read it quickly, and stuffed it into her pocket without saying a word. I was fascinated with the foreign-looking letter and dying to know what it said. "Is your father all right?" I asked.

"Papa is fine. I don't understand why I couldn't go to England with him. I wouldn't mind the bombs. I like dangerous things."

Danger, something else we couldn't provide on the island. The next stop was the grocery store. Besides groceries you could find toothpaste, playing cards, comic books (which Grandpa wouldn't let us buy), worms, and notebooks.

"So this is your cousin?" Mr. Brock said. "We'll just have to show her our welcome with a little present." He handed each of us a penny lollipop. We had been going to the store since we were babies, so Mr. Brock still thought of us as little kids.

I was horribly embarrassed when Carrie said, "No thanks."

Mr. Brock gave her a long look and then turned abruptly to wait on Mrs. Nelson from one of the other islands.

When we were outside, I said, "That was rude."

"I'm not going to be treated like a two-year-old," Carrie said.

"He was just being friendly. He gives all the kids suckers."

Carrie brightened when we got to the Norkins'. Mrs. Norkin had a large garden and sold vegetables and flowers from her front yard. On the days she worked for us on the island, Ned took over the stand. He was watching us come toward him.

He gave me a familiar grin, all the awkwardness of two nights before forgotten. He smiled at Carrie, too, but that smile had a lot more warmth to it. It didn't say, "Hey, here's old Belle again." It said, "Wow, this is a special day."

"Welcome to the Norkin emporium," Ned said. "What can I sell you? We've got diamonds, elephants, rainbows."

"Rhubarb and potatoes," I said, "and your mother said no green potatoes."

Ned gave me a withering look. "I offer you diamonds and you want potatoes."

Carrie was down on her knees smelling some plants Mrs. Norkin had potted up for sale. "Lavender!" She reached into her purse and pulled out a handful of bills. "I'll take five of these. We always had lavender in our garden in France."

Ned's eyes widened. "You lived in France?"

"*Certainement.*"

"And you speak French?"

"*Naturellement.* Would you like to learn French?"

"You can teach me French and I'll teach you to sail."

"Oh, I know how to sail. I'd love to go out with you though."

I scooped up the rhubarb and the potatoes. "We better be going," I said to Ned. "Your mom wants the rhubarb for a pie." My words came out sounding stiff and sour.

Ned left it to me to put everything into a brown paper bag while he carefully arranged the pots of lavender in a cardboard box for Carrie.

"*Au revoir*," Carrie said.

"Right," Ned said, never taking his eyes from her.

When we were back in the boat, Carrie said, "Your Ned's really *très charmant*."

"He's not *my* Ned," I snapped.

Carrie gave me a long look. "Sorry, I didn't know I was trespassing."

"I don't care," I lied. I didn't know whom to be more angry with, Carrie for flirting with Ned or Ned for falling all over her. Or worst of all, myself for caring so much.

After I delivered the groceries to Mrs. Norkin, I tramped over to the storm side of the island and spent an hour skipping stones on the lake. Grandpa had showed us how to pick out the flat oval stones and how to fling them out with a flick of your wrist so they skipped along the surface of the water. Grandpa could make a stone bounce along a dozen times. I loved the idea of a stone skimming over the water's surface, its heaviness bewitched away. My stones were sinking. I couldn't make them skip. I realized I was throwing the stones, wanting to hit something, and gave up.

When I returned to the cottage, I found Carrie had borrowed my best shorts and was out in the garden planting up the lavender. Grandma was standing alongside her, a big smile on her face.

"Belle, come here and see what Carrie is doing. I don't know why I never thought of lavender. It does so well in poor soil. Just smell that fragrance. It was so thoughtful of you, Carrie, but I'm not surprised. You're being your mother's daughter. I'm sure she had lavender. Your mother loved this garden. It was Julia's project. We should never have let it fall apart like this. It's just that working on it made me unhappy, it reminded me so of her." Grandma smiled. "You're like your mother, Carrie. It's almost like having Julia back."

Carrie stopped what she was doing and looked up at Grandma in surprise. Her face was flushed, and for a moment I thought I saw tears in her eyes. The next minute she was plunging the trowel into the ground as if she had something against the earth.

"I don't really remember my mother." Carrie patted the sandy soil in around the plants.

Grandma said, "One day we'll look for some pictures of Julia when she was your age, Carrie. I'm sure there must be some in the attic."

I left them and wandered up to my room feeling sorry for Carrie, making excuses for her because she had no mother. When I saw our room, my sympathy dwindled away. Carrie had flung her clothes every which way, leaving the room a complete mess. There was no corner of the room that she hadn't occupied. I knew that wolves peed on their territory to mark it as theirs. That seemed to be what Carrie was doing, marking my room for her own by putting her things in every corner. It was obvious that she was used to having someone pick up after her, but I wasn't going to be another Louise. I looked at the dress she had worn to the mainland. I had never in my whole life read someone else's mail, but I was so curious about Carrie, I couldn't resist. I reached into the dress pocket and pulled out the letter from her father. For a minute I guess I thought she was just another character in a book I was reading and the letter was another page to turn.

23 Park Lane
London, England

Ma chère Carrie,

I can speak freely about what is going on here in England, for this letter will avoid the British censors by crossing the ocean in a diplomatic pouch before it is mailed to you. I miss my Carrie very much, but it is a good thing you didn't come to England with me. Conditions here are very bad. There was great damage from the German bombs. Houses stand with their front walls missing and the furniture still in place like a scene from a play. Each day the English people must give up one more thing. There is little food and little fuel for heating homes. They still managed the races at Ascot, and of course I was there.

Happily there is a bit of good news from the battlefields. In Africa the British are beginning to chase the Germans, and over here General Eisenhower has just been put in charge of our American forces.

I hope things are going well for you. When your mother and I were first married, I visited Turtle Island, and I know how desolate it is and what a trial it must be for you to have to spend the summer there. I never understood why your mother loved it so. There is no civilization, only trees and stones. But just as the English are brave, so you must be brave as well and make the best of things.

You will find your grandfather a gruff old man, and I suppose your cousins run around the island like little sauvages. You will have to make allowances for them and get along with them as well as you can. It is only for one summer and then back to the beau monde.

I was too furious to read more. I put the letter back where I had found it. We were savages. There was no civilization on the island. Carrie was to suffer with us until she could get back to the *beau monde*, the fashionable world, as opposed to the trees and stones of the island. I longed to show the letter to Grandpa, "the gruff old man." Of course I couldn't. I wouldn't have hurt Grandpa's feelings for the world. Besides, he would be furious with me for reading someone else's letter. I was already furious with myself. I was even more furious with Carrie. She had been here only a few days and already Tommy and Emily had gotten into a fight, Nancy was refusing to play her recorder, Ned was acting like a sick cow, and now I had done something I was ashamed of doing.

After reading the letter, I didn't see how I was ever going to speak to Carrie again, let alone be nice to her. Yet I had to.

At dinner no one noticed how quiet I was. Grandpa was listening, fascinated, to Carrie's account of what her father had written about the effect of the war in England. I wondered what Grandpa would say if he knew how Uncle Howard had described him.

Grandma was going on about how perfect the lavender was for the garden. Emily was chattering about Carrie's having given her one of her velvet headbands to wear with her new pageboy. Nancy showed off the polish Carrie had put on her toenails. Mrs. Norkin was grinning because Carrie had said her rhubarb pie was *délicieuse*.

"Well," Grandma said, "there's a compliment for you, and the French certainly know good food."

Tommy said, "Then how come the French are dumb enough to eat snails and animal brains and stinky cheese?"

"Tommy, that's a very impolite thing to say," Grandma told him. "You should apologize to Carrie."

Carrie gave Tommy a sweet smile. "Oh, that's not necessary. I know he was just having a little fun."

Grandma patted Carrie's hand. "That's very generous of you, Carrie."

Even Grandma was taken in by Carrie.

I made some excuse about having a headache and skipping music practice, and I walked down to the lake. I didn't even have to look. I knew Ned would be out in the channel on his sailboat, and he was. I leaned as casually as I could manage against a tree and watched Carrie walk to the end of the dock and wave him in.

"Come and rescue me," she called.

When he made the boat fast to the dock, she said, "I'm not wearing heels tonight."

He grinned a foolish grin. "You're learning fast. Climb in." He spotted me. "Hey, Belle, want to come along?"

"Not tonight," I said.

He didn't coax me. Carrie said something I couldn't hear, and they both laughed. I didn't wait to watch them cast off. I turned toward the woods. Although the cottage was just down the path, the music sounded far away. I sulked because they were having their recorder session without me. I told myself it was my own fault, but that didn't help. I crushed some pine needles in my fingers and breathed in the fragrance. I didn't know how we would ever go back to being the way we were before Carrie came.

Five

The storm started in the late afternoon. The gulls had been shrieking all day. At breakfast Grandpa had pointed to the anvil-shaped clouds.

"A little weather on the way," he said.

Carrie looked up. "What kind of weather?"

"Thunderstorm." He looked at us kids. "Better keep close to the cottage. You don't want to be caught in the woods if there's lightning."

We had heard the warning a hundred times and paid no attention, but Carrie bit her lip and stared hard at Grandpa.

In the afternoon the sky turned a yellowish gray. There was a minute before the storm when everything was still: no birdsong, no wind, even the gulls hovered silently in the air like scraps of white paper. The world seemed to be holding its breath. Suddenly rain fell in gulps and splashes. Tommy, Emily, and I helped Grandpa drop the canvas curtain to keep the porch dry. Nancy, her wet hair plastered to her head, followed Polo in his mad dash for the house. Polo shook the water from his fur and with the first thunderclap slunk under the table.

After securing the porch, I stood at the living-room window. I loved the wildness of the storm, the sheets of water blowing across the channel, the wind whipping the cedars and bending the birch trees, the jagged spears of lightning splitting open the sky. I loved holding my breath and waiting for the thunder to follow the flash of lightning. The world was turned over to giants, nothing was small, everything that happened—the wind and lightning and thunder—was huge.

"Belle," Grandma said, "go upstairs and see what Carrie is doing. She seems to have disappeared."

I resented having to leave my post at the window to check on Carrie, who seemed to be letting us know over and over that she could take care of herself and didn't need us.

"I'll go," Emily volunteered.

"No, dear," Grandma told her, "Belle is going." I think Grandma was beginning to be a little bothered at the way Emily trailed after Carrie.

I trudged reluctantly up the stairs and pushed open the bedroom door. Carrie was on the bed, her knees drawn up close to her chest, her arms hugging her body. She was crying.

"Carrie! What's wrong?" I stood looking down at

her, afraid she had suddenly taken ill. "I'll get Grandma." I started for the door.

"No," she whispered. "I don't want anyone. Just leave me alone."

I sat down gingerly on the edge of her bed. Putting a hand on her shoulder, I begged, "Please, tell me what's the matter."

"It's the storm. The lightning will strike the cottage and we'll all be burned up."

I stared at her, unable to believe she could be so frightened, but she was. Storms on the island had always made me feel secure, as if the island were a refuge like Noah's ark.

I patted her shoulder, trying to calm her. "Grandpa has lightning rods on the roof, and anyhow there are tall trees on the island that would make a much better target than the cottage." I added, "I've seen worse storms than this one, lots worse."

Carrie sat up and looked at me. Her face was pale and her eyes huge. She didn't want to hear about storms that were "worse."

"Is it the island?" I asked. "Are you just afraid of being on the island?"

Carrie shook her head. "I hate storms. I had this awful nursemaid when I was little and we were living in France. She used to pull me into a closet with her to hide from the storms. She said the lightning could come through the windows even if they were closed. She said because I was such a bad girl, it would be sure to strike me. I hated her."

"Why didn't you tell your dad?"

"She said he wouldn't believe me, and he didn't until she broke my arm."

"Broke your arm!"

"I don't think she meant to, but I wouldn't do something she wanted me to, so she yanked me by the arm. It got twisted and broke. She told Papa I fell, but I screamed so loudly when she came near me, he got suspicious and sent her packing. I know it's silly, but I'm still afraid of storms." Carrie looked at me with a weak smile. "I've probably done enough bad things to deserve being punished with a bolt of lightning."

I remembered how when we kids had a toothache or a sore throat, or measles that itched like crazy, my mother would find something to take our minds off of our complaints.

"Carrie," I asked, "can I try on your dresses?"

Carrie looked at me as if I were pouring water on a drowning man. "Dresses! Now?"

"It's raining and there's nothing else to do. You don't have to pay attention."

"Do what you want to," Carrie said. Her voice was shaky. A bolt of lightning flashed across the sky. Seconds later there was a growl of thunder loud as a cage of lions. Carrie huddled into a ball.

I started for the closet. The first dress I pulled over my head was pink cotton with a white organdy collar. Carrie sat up in bed and stared at me.

"Not your style," she said. "I got it at Garfinkel's in Washington. I bought all my clothes there. Dad told Louise to use his charge account whenever I wanted something."

I tried to imagine what it would be like to go out and buy a dress "whenever I wanted." We were well enough off, but Emily and Nancy sometimes wore my hand-me-downs, and Mom dragged me around shopping for bargains. We were taught it was showing off to wear clothes that looked expensive. We wore clothes that no one would notice.

"Try on the one with the little yellow flowers— that's more your style." Carrie winced and ducked as a clap of thunder drowned out her last words, but she stayed sitting up.

The yellow dress was simple. I stood in front of the mirror thinking Carrie was right; it did look good on me. I looked like I wished I looked.

Carrie got off the bed. "Wait, there's an even better one."

Carrie had me try on all the dresses until there was only one left, an organdy dress with lilacs scattered over it. I could see the minute I took it off its hanger that it was much too small for me and would never fit Carrie.

She snatched it out of my hand. "Not that one. I'm saving it." She put the dress carefully back on the hanger. "In Paris Papa took me shopping at the Galeries Lafayette and bought the dress for me."

I didn't say anything, but I could tell from the careful way Carrie handled it that the dress must have been a special one because her father had bought it for her. It was her father and not the dress that was important to her. She had all those dresses, but that was all she had. She didn't have a mother, and her father was thousands of miles away.

"Carrie," I asked, "were all your nursemaids as awful as the one who broke your arm?"

"Oh, no. The ones in France were strict, but Louise is nice. She started working for us when we came back to this country. Anyhow, I never complained to Dad or he would have sent me to your family. Our grandmother and your mother were always sending letters to Dad saying they'd be glad to have me live with them. I know, because Dad kept the letters in his desk, and I read them."

So the nursemaid who broke her arm and the strict housekeepers were a lot better than living with us. Of course Carrie shouldn't have read her father's letters, but hadn't I done the same thing?

I had tried all the dresses on and Carrie was paying more attention to the storm. I couldn't believe that this was the same girl who claimed to like dangerous things and said she wouldn't be afraid of the bombs in England. The rain battered the windows. Lightning lit the sky, followed seconds later by thunder, and Carrie was folding herself up on the bed again. I felt sorry for her in a way I hadn't before.

Just then Emily burst into the room, a comb in one hand, a mirror in the other.

"Look, Carrie, the lemon juice must be working." Before the storm had come, Emily had been sitting in the sun with lemon juice on her hair hoping she would turn blond. "I'm sure there's the beginning of a lighter streak." She looked at Carrie. "Are you sick?"

Carrie sat up. "No, I'm fine." She tried a thin smile. She had let me see how frightened she was, but she wouldn't let Emily see. Emily's admiration was important to her. Emily looked up to Carrie, and Carrie wasn't going to let her down.

Suddenly Carrie stood up. She walked quickly to the closet and, pushing aside the other dresses, pulled out the dress her father had bought for her at Galeries Lafayette. She looked at it for a minute and then quickly handed it to Emily.

"Here—it's too small for me. You can have it."

Emily stared at the organdy dress, unable to believe it was hers. "Look, Belle," she said, "it's got a French label. It's from Paris!"

Six

For the next few days Carrie kept her distance from
me. I think she was ashamed of having let me see how
scared she had been of the storm. Emily shadowed
her just like Polo trailed after Nancy. Emily, with her
lemon juice and her pageboy and headband, her nail
polish and her garbling of French words picked up
from Carrie, was a smaller edition of Carrie.

Nancy was too busy with her own project to pay
much attention to Carrie. Nancy had discovered
heart-shaped tracks along the beach. From time to
time a deer would swim over to the island. Nancy was
putting out apple peels and corn to keep the animal
on the island. After exploring the beach each morning, she would run into the house to announce, "It's
still here!" She was so excited, you'd think it was a
unicorn.

Only Tommy said anything about Emily's imitat-
ing Carrie. I heard him tell Emily, "You're just like a

mockingbird. They spend all their time sounding like some other bird, so you never get to hear their own song, and their own songs are nicer than the songs of the birds they imitate."

I thought that was a compliment, but it made Emily angry.

"That's how much you know. You just don't appreciate elegance when it's right in front of you."

Eventually Emily might have tired of copying Carrie and gone back to being herself, but it happened faster than any of us could have guessed. It was one of those summer mornings when everything looks like it was poured out of a milk bottle. The water was a pale whitish blue. The sky was full of curdled white clouds. The freakish weather made me restless, so I was relieved when Grandma handed me my weekly list of things to get in Birch Bay. Carrie quickly volunteered to go with me. She took a long time to get ready. I guessed she hoped to run into Ned. Ned had come by nearly every night to take Carrie sailing. "She's terrific at crewing," he told me one evening when I was fishing off the dock and he was waiting for Carrie to join him. "When she was little, she used to go sailing with her dad off the coast of France. The Germans are there now." I had refused his invitations so many times, Ned no longer asked me if I wanted to go sailing with them.

I suppose I was jealous, so that afternoon when we were heading for the mainland, I took pleasure in waiting until after Carrie had done all her primping to mention casually that since it was one of the days Mrs. Norkin wasn't working for us, it would be Mrs. Norkin and not Ned who would be minding the vegetable and flower stand. "Ned probably will be off with his father guiding some fishermen." Carrie just shrugged.

As we anchored the boat, Carrie said, "I've got an errand in town. I'll meet you at the Norkins'."

By now the sun had burned off the clouds. It was July-hot out. Even walking the short distance down the main road to the Norkins' farm, I felt my damp shirt clinging to my back. In the winter when the city was all gray skies and wet slushy snow, I would dream of July days like this. The fields were gold with yellow mustard and the roadside blue with chicory. In the distance I could make out the Norkins' white farmhouse and red barn. The martins were swooping in and out of the holes in Mr. Norkin's purple martin house. When I got a little closer, I could see Mrs. Norkin fussing over her produce. She was particular about how the vegetables and flowers were displayed. There were freshly picked bouquets of cornflowers, marigolds, and sweet peas. Even the piles of beans and peas and lettuce were like paintings.

The minute she saw me, she called out. "Belle, I just baked some peanut butter cookies. They're your favorite."

I stood munching my second cookie while Mrs.

Norkin filled one of the used grocery store bags she saved with lettuce and radishes and three jars of her strawberry jam that was Grandpa's favorite.

"Where's your cousin today?" she asked.

"She'll be along. She stopped in town."

"That girl is a pretty enough thing, but she thinks we're all hicks."

It was like Mrs. Norkin to say what was on her mind. I felt I had to stick up for Carrie. She was family. "Oh, no," I said. "I think everything's just different for her."

Mrs. Norkin raised an eyebrow and, giving me one of the ironic looks she was famous for, said, "I hear she goes out sailing with Ned. I guess she's not above a little slumming if he wears a pair of pants."

So that was what made her critical of Carrie. She didn't like Carrie seeing Ned. Well, that was two of us.

Carrie appeared down the road making her way toward us from town. When you see someone suddenly, you look at them differently because you haven't gotten all your usual ideas together. Seen from a distance, Carrie'd lost her air of sophistication; she just looked like any girl. She was wearing a pair of my shorts and a shirt. For a minute I was confused. She looked like the cousin whom I had been expecting, the one I was going to be best friends with.

Mrs. Norkin must have seen what I did. "I guess she's just a kid," Mrs. Norkin said. "If she spends enough time with your family, she'll probably out-grow that fancy attitude."

I wasn't so sure. It was our attitudes, not Carrie's, that seemed to be changing.

I saw Carrie had a package, but I didn't think any-thing of it, guessing it would be lipstick or nail polish. She was on her best behavior, greeting Mrs. Norkin in a friendly way. She admired the bouquets on dis-play, and I saw Mrs. Norkin unbend a little.

"I've never seen such *bluets*," Carrie said.

"Those are cornflowers," Mrs. Norkin corrected Carrie.

"In France we call them *bluets*."

Mrs. Norkin's back was up. "Well, this is America, so they're cornflowers."

I felt a little sorry for Carrie. When we were settled in the runabout, I said, "I think *bluets* is a prettier name. I don't know why Mrs. Norkin didn't like it."

Carrie shrugged. "Like all the people around here, she's *une provinciale*."

A fancy French word for hick. Mrs. Norkin was right about Carrie. I didn't protest because I had let Carrie think I didn't know French. When she had asked me if I spoke it, I shook my head, afraid of her laughing at the way I garbled French words.

Carrie was in a good mood. Usually when I asked her about France, she shrugged and changed the sub-ject, so I had lost any hope of discovering what it was like. I thought that wasn't fair. Carrie had seen so much of the world, I didn't see why she wouldn't share it with me. This day she seemed eager to talk about France. It began with Mrs. Norkin.

"That woman," Carrie said, "thinks her little market is so special. Maurice, the chef at the American embassy, would take me with him to Les Halles early in the morning while it was still dark. There were blocks and blocks of vegetable and fruit markets, the tiniest beans like green threads, truffles worth their weight in gold, and *fraises de bois*, wild strawberries, no larger than my little fingernail. Or we'd go to the fish market and buy eels and sole flat as a pancake and piles of mussels and oysters."

Eels and mussels and oysters sounded disgusting to me, but I wanted Carrie to keep talking about Paris, so I tried to look like nothing would make me happier than swallowing a squirming eel followed by a slimy oyster.

"After we finished our shopping," Carrie said, "Maurice would take me with him to a little café to have onion soup with all the other chefs. You wouldn't believe who all would come and do their own shopping. The chef from the Ritz was actually there. Papa once took me to the Ritz for lunch. We ate in the garden room: cold lobster salad, and for dessert little chocolate soufflés. I've even had *escargots*, snails. Maurice said before you can eat the snails, you have to keep them inside the house and starve them for a couple of days, because they could have eaten something that wouldn't poison them but might poison you." When she saw the expression on my face, she laughed. "It isn't really the snails that are so good, it's the garlic and butter sauce they come with." Her mouth turned down and her eyes got watery. "Of course with the war, that's all gone. The *Boche* are in Paris now, and all the French are starving."

Carrie turned quiet. I couldn't get her to tell me more about Paris. When I asked her if she would like to go back there to live after the war, she only shook her head. "I don't know. It will all be so different. But of course if Papa goes, I must go, too."

I guided the runabout into its berth beside the dock. Before I could make the boat fast, Carrie scrambled onto the dock and ran up to the cottage. I saw Emily on the porch waiting for her. The screen door slammed shut, and the two of them disappeared up the stairway, giggling.

They stayed upstairs for the rest of the morning. Tommy and Nancy had made up a game. They had to walk around the living room on the furniture without touching the floor. Polo was trying to follow them. I rescued the vases as they toppled off the tables.

When Grandma called us for lunch, Carrie came down the stairs by herself, looking like I had never seen her look before, timid and defensive. She settled down on her chair keeping her head down.

"Where is Emily?" Grandpa asked. "She knows

it's lunchtime." Grandpa called up the stairway, "Young lady, we're waiting for you."

Several minutes went by while we all looked hungrily at the sandwiches Grandma had made with lots of mayonnaise and thick slices of Mrs. Norkin's bread and her watermelon pickles on the side. It was Grandpa's rule that no one touched a bite until everyone was at the table.

Finally Emily slipped into her chair. Her eyes were red and she was wearing a cotton sun hat with her hair tucked up into the hat.

"Whatever is the matter, dear?" Grandma asked.

Emily shook her head. Nothing we said could get her to say a word. She tore her sandwich into bits and nibbled on a pickle. We pretended everything was all right and talked with one another, but neither Emily nor Carrie said a word.

As soon as lunch was over, Emily shot a furious glance at Carrie and ran outdoors. Carrie went up to our bedroom and shut the door. It was our time for reading. I took my book and set off after Emily. I knew her favorite place just as she knew mine. I headed for a grove of cedars not far from the cottage. For some reason the cedars had formed a kind of circle. Nancy called it a fairy ring and always checked it on the night of a full moon to see if there were any signs of fairies dancing. Inside the ring of trees was a small circle of grass where Emily liked to curl up and read, pleased to be so close to everyone but still invisible.

I found her sobbing.

"Em, what is it?" As I put my arms around her, her sun hat fell off. "Oh! Em!" Her hair was the brassy orange-yellow of an egg yolk. "What happened to you!"

She was sobbing harder than ever. I could just make out her words. "She did it. I wanted blond hair like hers, and she said she would bleach it."

I knew now what Carrie had bought in Birch Bay. Bleach for Emily's hair. "It will grow out," I promised Emily.

She wiped her eyes and snuffled. "It'll take forever. It was awful when I looked in the mirror. It's not me anymore. She's taken me away. I hate her for doing that to me."

"Carrie didn't mean it to turn out like that. She feels as bad as you do."

It was late afternoon before I could calm Emily down enough to get her into the cottage and up to her bedroom. When I brought Grandma up to see Emily, she was horrified.

"That was a thoughtless thing for Carrie to do," Grandma said. "She's older than Emily and should have known better." It was the first criticism of Carrie I had heard Grandma make.

She tried to comfort Emily. "We'll have it cut short, dear, and by the time the summer is over, it'll be mostly grown out."

Emily refused to go into Birch Bay to the barbershop. Instead she let Grandpa cut it.

"Nothing to it," he said. "I used to help shear the sheep on the farm when I was a boy." He tried to make a joke out of it, but I could see he was angry with Carrie.

"You were very foolish, Carrie," he told her.

This time Carrie didn't answer back. She stood there rigid and silent, as if at the least movement she would break apart. Later I found her in our room looking miserable. "No matter what I do," she said, "it's the wrong thing. Emily begged me to bleach her hair. I thought I was doing her a favor. She was the only one of you who liked me, and now she hates me."

"She doesn't hate you—she's just disappointed. She'll get over it. And as for her being the only one of us who likes you, that's not true. We all like you. Just give us a chance." I took a deep breath. "I like you. Honest."

Carrie gave me a searching look. I have to admit I'm not too good at hiding my feelings, but at that moment, if I didn't exactly like Carrie, I felt sorry for her. I guess that was enough for her, because she gave me a weak smile.

Emily kept to herself, curled up on the porch swing with a book or hidden away in the birch circle. We all tried not to look at her hair, pretending we had just met one another and were showing off how polite we were.

Tommy couldn't stand the gloom that had settled

over everyone. The second day in the middle of lunch he said in a loud voice, "I don't see why it's such a big deal. Goldfinches are bright yellow all summer, and then in the fall they turn a brownish green."

We all stared at him. Only Tommy would compare Emily to a goldfinch. I couldn't keep a straight face. Grandma and Grandpa started to laugh.

Emily glowered at Tommy. "I'm not a goldfinch," she said. A minute later she was smiling. Suddenly all the tension was gone. We knew one day this would just be the summer Carrie bleached Emily's hair and it would be a family joke, something to make us all laugh. We were back together again, and even Carrie smiled.

Seven

July smothered us. It was hot every day, and at night the bedroom curtains never stirred. Emily, Nancy, and Polo spent nights in the upstairs sleeping porch. Tommy slept in the porch downstairs. Carrie tossed restlessly in her bed.

Our days were back to normal: early-morning dips in the lake, rebuilding the log cribs, reading in the afternoon, going along with Nancy's schemes. As she usually did every summer after the first excitement of planting some flowers, Emily forgot about the garden. Without saying a word to anyone, Carrie took over. We all saw she was trying to make up for the damage she had done with the bleach. She was in the garden every afternoon on her knees, doing Emily's job for her, pulling out weeds around the marigolds and lavender plants. The lavender plants were thriving in the poor soil, spreading out into a small hedge.

Carrie never went swimming or helped with the stones. If she wasn't sitting on the dock, her arms around her knees, staring out at the water, she kept to her room, reading her magazines, writing letters, lounging on her bed complaining about the heat. She might as well have been in some apartment in the middle of a city instead of on an island.

At first I hadn't paid any attention to the letters to her father. She wrote them in French and left them lying on the dresser. I was sure that when I had said I didn't speak French, she had understood that to mean that I didn't know French. My curiosity got the better of me. I didn't exactly read the letters. I walked by the dresser as if the letters weren't someone I planned to meet, but just ran into. Certain phrases caught my eye. *"Je suis une prisonniere,"* I'm a prisoner. *"La cuisine est piteuse,"* the food is pitiful. That wasn't a big shock. Carrie had let us know how she felt about being with us and eating our pitiful food. Of course I looked to see what she thought of everyone. Grandfather was *l'ancien*, the old one. Nancy was *l'amusette*, a toy. Ned was *très agréable*, very agreeable. I was *une solitaire*, a hermit, a recluse, or it could mean a lonely person, which wasn't far off the mark. I had lost Ned, and Carrie didn't seem to want to have anything to do with me.

Some things in the letters were sad. Carrie begged her father to let her come to London. She wrote that she would take care of him and would keep him from *le péril*, danger, and *les bombes*, the bombs. *Grandmère*, she said, had told her she was like her mother. *"Est-ce que c'est vrai?"* she asked her father. Is it true? My conscience got the better of me and I stopped reading the letters. Carrie's letters to her father were the only way she could have a private conversation with him. I knew I would hate to have her listening in to what I said to my father in confidence. Anyhow, I didn't see what I could do about what I discovered.

In the evenings Carrie went sailing with Ned. The rest of us, after our recorder session, played cards or listened to the war news. In the Soviet Union six thousand German and Russian tanks were battling one another. The war had found its way across the ocean and even onto our island. Only the week before, the Birch Bay weekly newspaper had had an article about a local soldier who had been killed. Carrie said Ned was still planning to join up in the spring. I hated hearing about Ned's plans from Carrie when it should have been me out there who Ned was confiding in.

One evening, watching Carrie head for the dock and Ned's sailboat, Grandma asked me, "Why don't you go with them?"

I shook my head. "I'm in the middle of an exciting chapter." I grabbed a book from a pile on a chair and headed for the porch.

Grandma followed me. "Belle, you haven't been your usual cheerful self. Is something wrong?"

I shook my head.

"Are you getting along with Carrie?"

I shrugged.

"Carrie's life has been so different from the life that we lead here. Changing has been a hard adjustment for her."

"She's changing *us*. We're the ones who are different since she came. She's just the same."

Grandma gave me one of her thoughtful looks. "Maybe we're too isolated here on the island, Belle. Maybe it's not a bad thing to learn to live with people who are a bit different than we are."

Though our routines were the same, there were changes. Grandpa seemed bewildered by all the small rebellions that were going on: Emily's staying in bed in the morning, Nancy skipping our recorder practice, Tommy's growing stubbornness, and my sulks. I don't think Grandpa connected the changes with Carrie. I think he believed we were all getting up on the wrong side of the bed or had come down with some temporary mind flu from which we would soon recover. Grandpa believed in things being neat and tidy, and if they weren't, you just waited ten minutes and everything would get back to normal because that's the way the world was meant to be—orderly.

Grandma was different. She wasn't seeing Carrie at all. She was seeing someone else who wasn't here. She was seeing Aunt Julia. In Grandma's eyes, with

Carrie there, Grandma had her daughter back, so Carrie could do no wrong.

Our friends on the other islands hadn't met Carrie. We hadn't made our usual weekly trip to the Lodge for dinner because Grandma believed it was better for Carrie to get used to us before she had to meet all the other families. Finally Grandpa announced that we would have dinner on Big Island.

Carrie perked right up. She ran up the stairs to our bedroom and began pulling dresses out of the closet. I watched for a few minutes. "Dinners at the Lodge are really informal," I said. "No one dresses up."

"I don't suppose they'll refuse to feed me if I wear something decent. What is there about these islands that makes everyone want to look grubby?"

I headed for the channel with a bar of Ivory soap. By the time I got back to our room, Carrie was all dressed. I had to admit that with every hair of her pageboy in place and a white lace blouse and flowered cotton skirt, she looked terrific, like something right out of *Mademoiselle*. I slipped on the only dress I had packed, a faded cotton one with a torn pocket and an ink stain. I guess I was in a growing phase, because the dress was suddenly too short for me.

Carrie gave me an amused look. "You looked great in that yellow dress of mine. You're welcome to wear it."

I longed to put on her dress, but I was too proud—

or too stubborn. I shook my head, tucked my wet hair behind my ears, and rubbing away the sand between my toes, got into my worn sandals. When I caught a glimpse in the mirror of the two of us side by side, I had to admit that I took some sick satisfaction in my pathetic appearance, as if points were given out for looking grubby.

"I don't understand," Carrie said, "why I'm supposed to let your family keep giving me everything like I was Little Orphan Annie and no one will let me give anything back."

"Sold," I said. "Hand me the yellow dress." When I stole a look in the mirror, I looked like I belonged with Carrie, not like her sister sitting home among the ashes. In the reflection Carrie and I both had big smiles on our faces.

The runabout couldn't hold the whole family, so Grandpa ran his Chris-Craft out of the boathouse. It was one of the early models from the twenties. No one was allowed to take it out except Grandpa, and he almost hated to get it wet.

It was only a short ride to Big Island and the Lodge. The Lodge was where all the island people who owned cottages on the islands got together. There were tennis courts and even a croquet lawn. There were swings and slides for the little kids, who played outside with their nursemaids and ate at a separate little kids' table. Before the war put a stop to it, there were dances with a real orchestra.

The clubhouse itself was a big old wooden building with a wide porch and a dock large enough to accommodate several boats. It was furnished with old-fashioned comfortable sofas and chairs with sagging seats. If you reached under one of the cushions, along with a lot of crumbs you'd probably find someone's sunglasses and a grocery list. The little kids always looked for pennies. Magazines like *Vogue* and *Yachting*, most of them a couple of years old, were strewn on the tables. On cool nights there was a fire in the big stone fireplace. On this warm night the windows were all open, and a channel breeze fluttered the curtains.

A couple dozen resorters were gathered for dinner. We knew all of them, though there were guests we hadn't met before. The Adamses, an elderly couple, were there with their houseful of grandchildren, who burst into the clubhouse like a bunch of puppies let out of a kennel. Everyone was happy to see the Wallaces back. There had been a rumor over the winter that Mrs. Wallace was in the hospital with something serious. The Nelsons were there from Chicago with their son, Brad, who was standing a little apart looking like he wanted to be a million miles away. He was movie-star handsome and knew it. For as long as I could remember, he'd always turned up with something he ought not to have, like cigarettes when he was twelve, and once at a Fourth of July celebration a really dangerous firecracker.

My sisters and brother gravitated toward friends their ages. Grandma was taking Carrie around introducing her to everyone. I tracked down Marcia Adams, one of the Adamses' grandchildren.

Marcia was shorter than I was, with clipped black curly hair and green eyes that didn't miss anything. She was as good as a newspaper. "Betty Hurd is getting married. Wait until you see the lucky man. He looks like his suit is three sizes too small for him and his eyes bulge. Jimmy flunked sixth grade, sixth grade! The Fraziers had a big fight. You could hear them clear out in the channel. The club's having chicken again tonight, and apple pie with ice cream. What happened to Emily's hair? Is that blonde who looks like a magazine cover your cousin?"

"Yes." Carrie was talking with Brad Nelson.

"I heard Brad was thrown out of his high school for drinking," Marcia whispered.

I stole a glance in their direction. Carrie and Brad were standing close to each other. They would look in the direction of someone, lean toward each other, whisper something, and laugh.

Grandma noticed it too. As we sat down for dinner, she turned to Carrie. "You and the Nelson boy seemed to be getting along."

"He asked me to come over to their cottage. I guess he can't come to see us. Maybe he can't use their boat."

Grandpa looked up from cutting up Nancy's

chicken for her. "Probably not Mr. Nelson's boat. Mr. Nelson has one of the first Chris-Craft they made, a 1924 model. It's older than mine. Mr. Nelson and I have spent a lot of summers together restoring our boats."

"Why would someone spend so much time on an old boat?" Carrie asked.

Grandpa looked as startled as if Carrie had asked why the sun shone. "Why would someone want an old painting by Rembrandt? Those boats are master-pieces."

"So that's why Brad has no boat to use."

"No." Grandpa frowned. "They also have a run-about like ours. I think it has something to do with where he goes with a boat."

"Belle could take me over to see him," Carrie said.

"I'm afraid that boy has been in some trouble," Grandpa said. "Let's give him a little time to get back on the proper track. Anyhow, in my day girls didn't go running after boys."

Carrie looked hurt, and Grandma quickly said, "I don't know about that, Everett. I had my eye on you long before you noticed me."

There was a lot of laughter, and nothing more was said about Carrie visiting the Nelsons. Dinner was nearly over. Nancy was fighting off Tommy's fork. He was snatching pieces of her apple pie. Grandma was using a napkin and ice water to rub away a gravy stain on Emily's dress. Marcia was signaling to me across the dining room to see her after dinner was over.

Grandpa didn't have a lot of patience for sitting around chatting. He was always impatient to get back to the island. As soon as we finished dessert, Grandpa and Grandma began saying their good-byes. Carrie and Brad walked out on the dock, talking to each other. I hurried to find Marcia.

"Guess what?" she asked. "I overheard your glamorous cousin and Brad Nelson talking about going to the Shanty."

There was no time for questions. Grandpa was calling me. I was sure Marcia was mistaken. Brad must have been telling some wild story about the Shanty—and there were lots of such stories. The Shanty was an all-night bar about five miles east of Birch Bay on the water, a place where loggers and fishermen and their dates hung out. On weekends there was a local band and dancing. I couldn't believe that Brad would ever set foot in a place like that, and anyhow, he couldn't take out a boat, so there would be no way to get there.

On the way back to the island Tommy begged Grandpa to slow down so he could see an osprey's nest. The nest, on the top of a tall pine tree, looked like someone had thrown together a pile of sticks. The huge brown-and-white bird peered down at us but never moved from its nest.

Tommy was excited. "They've got two fledglings," he said.

"What do you think of that, Caroline?" Grandpa asked.

"Amazing," Carrie said, but even though she was looking right at the nest, I don't think she saw it.

Eight

The next day a miracle occurred. Carrie was out of bed and in her bathing suit, her hair pinned up, ready to jump into the lake with the rest of us. She was in and out of the water in a minute. "Felt great," she called over her shoulder, running back to the house. After lunch she said, "I'll go with you, Belle, when you go over to Birch Bay."

Grandma said, "While you're there, girls, why don't you stop by the Norkins' and get us some lettuce and spinach if it hasn't bolted. Be sure not to use up any more gas in the boat than you absolutely need. Our coupons are nearly gone for this month."

In the past I'd had to remind Carrie to cast off the aft line, but this afternoon she moved quickly, tossing the line into the runabout. "I've been such a drag," she said. "I really want to learn how to do all the things you do, Belle. I'd love to learn how to run the boat."

Before I thought how rude it would sound, I said, "Grandpa would never let you."

Carrie flushed. "I'm older than you and I'm not exactly stupid. I don't know why I shouldn't be able to learn."

"It's just that I've been around boats all my life," I said, trying to sound a little more polite. "I didn't mean you couldn't learn."

"Never mind," Carrie said. "I don't know why I even try. You'll never let me be a part of this family."

I felt guilty. She had jumped into the water in the morning with the rest of us. "We're going to Birch Bay this afternoon. Maybe on the way home," I said, half hoping she would have forgotten by then. As we passed the other islands, Carrie asked, "Where's the Nelsons' place?"

"Over there," I said, pointing to a large gray cottage. Carrie stared at it but didn't say anything.

On the mainland Carrie offered to get the mail while I picked up the coffee Mr. Brock had been keeping for us under the counter. Coffee was nearly impossible to get during the war, but Mr. Brock and Grandpa were old friends. Carrie had a letter to mail, and I assumed it was to her father. She was waiting for me when I came out of the store. At the Norkins' farm we found Ned changing a tire on his dad's truck.

"No way are we going to be able to get new tires until the war is over," he said. "I'll just have to keep patching them." He smiled at both of us, but he couldn't take his eyes off Carrie. "What can I do for you?" he asked.

"Just stuff to graze on," I said. I filled one bag with lettuce and another with spinach.

Carrie was looking over the plants for sale, paying no attention to Ned. "What's this plant with all the tiny white flowers? It's so airy and delicate."

Ned walked over to her. "That's a great description. It's baby's breath." He waited a minute. "I'll be over to take you sailing tonight, Carrie."

Carrie glanced at him as if she had never seen him before. "I've got stuff to do tonight," she said.

I knew that she didn't have anything to do and that she was just putting Ned off, but Ned had no clue.

He asked, "Well, let's do it tomorrow night."

"Sorry," she said, and nothing more.

I cringed as I watched Ned realize she was telling him she didn't want to see him, tonight or tomorrow night or ever. Now that she had met Brad, she didn't care about Ned. Brad was more exciting, more big city. Ned was just a small-town boy who sold vegetables and moved luggage.

Bewildered, he turned to me like you reach for a life preserver. "Belle?"

"Sure. Come by after supper." I know I should have resented being his second choice, but he looked so devastated. I think at that moment I was angrier at Carrie for what she was doing to Ned than for all the trouble she was causing our family.

Carrie scooped up a couple of pots of baby's breath, paid Ned as if he were some shopkeeper she had never seen before, and headed for town.

As we climbed into the runabout, Carrie watched me cast off the mooring lines. As soon as we were clear of the dock, she asked again, "Why can't I try driving or running the boat or whatever you call it?"

Ever since we had left the island that afternoon, there had been something in the back of my head, something that had been trying to escape like one of those laboratory rats that keep running back and forth in a maze hunting for a way out. I knew what it was now. Carrie wanted to take the runabout to Brad Nelson's cottage. She wanted him to take her to the Shanty. She wanted excitement. I knew perfectly well that Grandpa would have a fit if Carrie took the runabout. I told myself that at last he and Grandma would see Carrie for what she was, a selfish, spoiled creature. He'd send her away and our family could go back to being what we were before Carrie came and ruined everything.

I moved over to make room for Carrie. "Okay, you take the controls. The first thing you have to do is start the blower to get rid of gas fumes. That's crucial. Wait a couple of minutes. Turn it off and start the ignition." As we swung out into the channel, there was a flush of excitement on Carrie's face.

Alarmed, I shouted, "Not so fast. And watch out.

You have to stay inside the buoys, or you'll run the boat over a boulder or get hung up on the shoals." I saw that Carrie, in her excitement at handling the boat, wasn't paying attention to what I was saying. "Carrie, listen, this is important. You have to keep inside the buoys. Remember to keep the red buoys on your left. Then when you're heading into the harbor at Birch Bay, they'll be on your right."

"What about at night?"

"Well, in the summer it's light until nearly eleven. Anyhow, we're never out that late."

"But if you were?"

Of course I knew what she was thinking. I should have stopped the whole plan right then and there. I only said, "People around here just know the channel, even in the dark."

When we were in sight of the cottage, I pushed her aside and took over the controls.

"Grandpa might see us," I warned.

Carrie moved over, but the look of excitement stayed.

For the next few days things were quiet. Carrie went back to sleeping in mornings. Nancy was busy building furniture for her dolls out of twigs. Tommy had discovered an indigo bunting nest. Emily was as excited as Tommy. "It's the most gorgeous shade of blue," she said. "There's blue inside the blue."

On Sunday Grandpa built a bonfire on the beach to fix his specialty, planked whitefish. He had learned how to do it from an Indian he had known when he and Grandma had first come to the islands. He got out his oak board, smoky smelling and singed and brown from past fires. He laid fillets of the whitefish he had caught that afternoon on the plank. Bacon slices went over the fillets. Grandpa tapped nails through the slices and the fillets. On the beach he built a fire in front of a large boulder that he used to prop up the board. The heat from the fire cooked the whitefish while the fat from the bacon basted it.

It took about an hour to cook, and while we waited, growing hungrier and hungrier, Grandpa told us the latest war news.

Discussions about the war made Carrie restless. "Why do people have to talk about the war all the time?" she asked. I knew she was thinking about her father. In the last few days Germany had increased its bombing of England. There were more casualties. A couple of nights ago, when we had all gathered around the radio to hear the news from England, Carrie had hurried out of the room.

Seeing how Carrie had been affected by the broadcast, Grandma had said, "Everett, maybe we ought to give up listening to the war news."

Grandpa had frowned. "Of course we can't give up listening. There's a war on. It's our duty to know what's going on. We may be on an island, but our men are out there giving their lives; the least we can do is be aware of their sacrifices." But after that

Grandpa waited until we were all in bed to listen to the war news. I could hear the radio crackling, the volume turned low, as it whispered softly to Grandpa.

Now Grandpa said, "You're right, Caroline—there must be something more cheerful to talk about. Tommy, why don't you tell us about the whistling swans you saw this morning?"

Tommy was eager to describe waking up to strange *woo hoo* sounds. "I could hear them a long time before they settled down on the channel. There must have been a dozen of them." Whistling swans were rare; you only saw them migrating through, and all day Tommy had gone around with a small smile on his face as if he had been let in on a wonderful secret.

Grandma told a story about black swans. "All the black swans in England are owned by the king. There is a man who works for the crown whose job it is to travel the rivers and count the black swans."

"Do you have to be English to do that?" Tommy asked. We could all see he would love the job.

Emily described a strange duck she had seen. "Its face was painted white and black in a funny pattern, like a clown."

"Wood duck," Tommy said. Carrie appeared to be listening to us, but you could see her mind was on something else. I wondered if it might be her father. I missed my own dad a lot, but I heard from him every week and I knew he was safe in an office only a few hours away from us.

When the whitefish was done, Grandpa divided it up and presented a portion to each of us with a flourish.

"It's very good," Carrie told Grandpa when she tasted the whitefish, but that wasn't compliment enough for Grandpa, who was used to raves for his planked whitefish. He covered his disappointment, but we could see his feelings were hurt.

Carrie saw it too. Later that night when we were getting ready for bed, she said, "I guess I should have said more about Grandpa's whitefish. I was thinking of something else."

"Your dad?" I asked.

Carrie was silent for a moment and then said, "Yes, I was thinking of Papa."

Nine

The next afternoon Grandpa took the little runabout to the mainland to pick up letters. He would have liked to take his Chris-Craft with its polished Philippine mahogany planking that gleamed in the sun, but the Chris-Craft used more gas than the smaller boat. When he returned, he passed out the letters, handing one to Carrie. He glanced at the return address. "Brad Nelson. Looks like you've made a conquest, Caroline. I hope for the Nelsons' sake that that young man pulls himself together." Carrie took the letter and hurried up to our room. Grandpa looked after her for a minute and then, shrugging his shoulders, asked, "Who's going to help me bury the garbage?"

Grandpa heaved a shovel over his shoulder like a soldier marching off to war. Emily, Nancy, and Tommy marched along behind him, each lugging a bag of onion and potato peels and other disgusting stuff that had to be buried. Stones would be placed over the burial spots so raccoons and skunks couldn't dig it up. Nancy convinced Grandpa to let her scatter some of the garbage for the animals. "A little doesn't hurt," she pleaded. I begged off, and the raggle-taggle army, busy with their errand, went on without me.

I wandered down to the dock, picking my way quickly over boards hot from roasting all morning in the sun. I stuck my feet in the channel's clear water to cool off. I could see a school of silver minnows flashing first one way and then another. A silent message of bubbles percolated up from a clamshell. A crab scuttled by looking like a dead hand. Farther out a gull dove at the water and came up with a small fish in its mouth. I counted the days on my fingers until Carrie would go back to Washington. I didn't see how I could put up with her. My room was always a mess—her clothes spilling out of the drawers, her makeup taking up every inch of dresser space, the floor cluttered with piles of stupid magazines. There was nothing left of me in the room. I felt I was disappearing.

Tommy had left a fishing pole on the dock. I reached down for the minnow trap and captured one of the tiny silver fish. I hooked the minnow and cast out. Though it was hard to keep my mind on fishing, I felt like I had to do something or burst. On the third cast I hooked a good-size perch. I debated throwing it back. The rule was whoever got the fish had to scale and clean it, a job I hated. I kept it and the next five perch I caught. Grandma would fry them for breakfast in the morning. Four of the perch were in the water on the stringer; the last one was thrashing around on the dock. I headed for the boathouse to get the scaler and the gutting knife. There was a light on. The light came from the runabout. It was immediately switched off. I saw a figure scramble out of the boat. It was Carrie. She must have entered from the door on the other side of the boathouse.

"What are you doing?" I demanded.

"Nothing. Now that you're letting me handle the runabout, I just thought I'd get familiar with all the switches."

"Well, the running lights are for fog or dark, and I'm not allowed to take the boat out then. Actually you shouldn't be touching the boat at all."

"You don't have to worry," Carrie said. "I'm not hurting Grandpa's precious boat." She ran out, upsetting an empty gasoline can next to the runabout and slamming the door behind her.

I stood there forgetting all about the fish that was slowly cooking in the sun. I had been right. Carrie planned to take the boat out so she could see Brad, maybe even pick him up and go over to the Shanty with him. I knew what I should do—tell Grandpa. Of course she would deny it and I had no way of proving it. That didn't matter. I still had to tell. Carrie didn't know the channel well enough to take the boat out at night.

If I said nothing and she took out the boat, Grandpa might send her back to her precious Louise and we could all get back to normal. The summer wouldn't be entirely spoiled. But if something happened to her? What then? Standing there in the murky light of the boathouse, I put together a plan. I would pretend to be asleep. When I heard her get up I would watch out the window. The minute I saw the boat I'd awaken Grandpa and I'd tell him. He would go right after her with the Chris-Craft. It was much faster. He'd catch her up in no time and bring her back. Then she'd have to leave. It seemed so simple. I told myself I was doing what was good for the whole family.

I went back to the dock. After the shadowy boathouse the bright sun made me blink. I felt as if I had been in the boathouse for a long time, but it could only have been a minute or two, for the perch was still slapping its tail against the dock. I picked it up to slam it against a board but something made me stop. After a minute I slid it back into the water. I hauled up the stringer and let the other four fish go too. I think I wanted to do something kind, something good. I think I wanted to even things out.

That night Carrie didn't put her hair up in curlers, didn't slosh goo on her hands and put on her white gloves. As soon as she climbed into bed, she gave a great yawn, turned down her lamp, and slid under the covers. I did the same.

Lying there awake, I could feel her like something light balanced in the air, just waiting to fall to the ground. Emily, Tommy, and Nancy were already asleep. I heard Grandpa listening to the eleven-o'clock news, and then he and Grandma came up the stairway and went into their room. Their bedroom door closed.

All the while I was lying there, I was changing my mind back and forth. The minute Carrie got out of bed, I could threaten to tell on her. That would end her adventure. Of course she would hate me, but if I waited until after she left, she might never know how Grandpa found out.

I heard Carrie get up and slip into her clothes. I could feel her breath as she bent over me to be sure I was asleep. I didn't move, keeping my breathing regular. Through half-closed eyes I saw her tiptoe out of the room holding her shoes. She went down the stairway so carefully there wasn't even a creak. She must have practiced. I ran to the window. The moon was nearly full, and I could see her crossing the yard and running down to the boathouse. She disappeared inside. Now, I thought, now is the time I should call Grandpa. I waited another minute. The runabout moved out into the channel, its light making a narrow road of gold on the water.

"Grandpa," I called. "Grandpa, wake up quick! Carrie's gone. She took the runabout. I saw her from the window."

My shout awakened everyone. Polo was running back and forth barking. Grandpa came out into the hallway in his blue striped pajamas. Grandma had thrown a robe over her nightie; her hair was neatly caught up in a net. Nancy, Emily, and Tommy stood in the hallway, half asleep.

I wanted Grandpa to start out at once. It worried me that he was just standing there. If he waited much longer, it would be hard to catch Carrie up.

"Mirabelle, what are you talking about?"

I repeated my story about hearing some noise and finding Carrie gone. "I looked out of the window, and I saw Carrie running down the path. Then I saw the runabout come out of the boathouse. You have to go after her in the Chris-Craft. She doesn't know the channel."

"There's no gas in the Chris-Craft. I left the can in the boathouse. I was going to take the runabout in tomorrow and get some." Grandpa looked at me. "When did Caroline learn to use the runabout?"

I was too upset not to tell the truth. "I taught her."

Grandfather was staring hard at me. "Without my permission!"

I nodded.

Everything had fallen apart. Grandpa couldn't go after Carrie. She was alone out there in the dark. It was all my fault. "I think she was going to see Brad," I mumbled. "Maybe they were going to the Shanty."

Grandpa was still looking at me. "If you knew all

this, why didn't you say something, Mirabelle?"

"I wasn't sure." One word stuck to the other.

"Oh, Belle," Grandma said, but her look said a lot more.

I ran into my room and threw myself onto my bed, sobbing. Nothing Carrie had done was as bad as what I had done. I saw the runabout crashing into a boulder or running aground on a shoal. I saw her alone on the channel in the dark, the boat sinking.

Grandpa pounded down the steps. Grandma came into my room and sat down beside me on the bed.

"It's my fault. I could have stopped her. What if she drowns?"

"Your grandfather's got the canoe out. He's going to paddle over to the clubhouse and use their phone to call Mr. Norkin. Mr. Norkin will come and pick your grandfather up. They're certain to find Carrie. I'm sure she'll be all right—she's a resourceful young woman—but Belle, whatever were you thinking of to teach her to use the boat and then to let her go out at night alone?"

"She's changed all of us," I blurted out. "I would never have done something like that before Carrie came."

Grandma spoke in a quiet voice. "Carrie doesn't have the power to change any of us. Carrie didn't make you behave in this thoughtless way. You have to take responsibility for your own actions, Belle. Carrie did a foolish and dangerous thing, but you not only let Carrie do it, you made it possible for her to do it." Grandma went out of the room and closed the door behind her. It was as if she had shut me away from the whole human race.

From the same window I had watched Carrie take off in the runabout, I watched Grandpa maneuver the canoe out into the channel. The pale light of the moon turned Grandpa and the canoe into something vague and blurred, something that might melt right before my eyes.

Downstairs I heard everyone moving around and talking. I didn't want to face them, but I had to know what was happening. I went slowly down the stairway. Emily and Tommy were in chairs, their feet drawn up under them. Nancy, half asleep, was on the davenport leaning against Polo. I could hear Grandma in the kitchen. She appeared with glasses of milk and a plate of cookies.

Grandma passed around the glasses of milk. Her hand was shaking. When she came to me, I said, "no thanks," but she held a glass out to me anyhow. "It may be a long wait, Belle; you'll feel better with something in your stomach." Half to herself she said, "I don't know what Howard will say when he hears about this business."

I knew Grandma was thinking that Uncle Howard had sent Carrie to us to be safe from the bombs in England. Now, because of what I had let happen, she was in danger. I put my glass of milk down on the table. I couldn't choke a drop down my throat.

Grandma tried to get Nancy and Tommy and Emily to go back to bed, but they refused. "I wouldn't feel right," Emily said. "I haven't been very nice to her."

I stared at a framed map of the islands that had hung on the wall as long as I could remember. One summer the rain had leaked down that wall and left a stain on the map. Silently I traced the path Carrie might have taken. Although I could have followed the path in my sleep, still I studied the map as if the route through the channel to Brad's house might have changed since the day before. If you stayed within the buoys, you were all right, but at night they were difficult to see. Several boulders and a small sandbar lay just outside the buoys. If Carrie was going fast and hit a boulder, she could knock a hole in the runabout. It was twenty feet to shore. I had only seen her jump in and out of the water and didn't even know if she could swim. I tried to remember if they had a lake near Paris or Washington where she might have learned to swim. I wondered why I hadn't thought to teach her.

Nancy had fallen asleep next to Polo. He lay still, but his eyes were open and his ears stuck up. I started to chew on my nails. I hadn't done that since Mom had taken me for a real manicure in sixth grade.

Grandma was sitting down with her hands folded, and I wondered if she was saying a prayer and if I should, too. I wanted to ask God to keep Carrie safe, but I was afraid to call God's name. I was afraid to have him notice me.

Polo heard it first. He began to bark. If it had been during the day, he would have paid no attention; the sound of boats on the channel was no more uncommon than the sound of the gulls. Now we all looked at one another. I was the first one up and out of the cottage. I felt the sharp prick of the gravel path under my bare feet. I got there just as Mr. Norkin was throwing a line over the post on the dock. Grandpa and Carrie were in the boat with him.

"Well, here she is," Mr. Norkin said, "just a little the worse for wear."

Carrie was huddled in the back of the boat. Grandpa reached over and, taking her hand, helped her out onto the dock. She was carrying her shoes, and the hem of her skirt was wet and clinging to her legs. Grandma put an arm around her.

Mr. Norkin explained. "I picked up Everett at the club, and we found the runabout stuck on that shoal over near Birch Island. She'd climbed out of the boat and was trying to push it off the sandbar. Good thing she didn't succeed. If the boat had got loose, she'd never have gotten back in it." Mr. Norkin looked around at our worried faces. I guess he decided he wanted to get out of there before the questions started. He reached for the line Grandpa had just fastened and unhitched it. "Well," he said, "it's past my bedtime. I'll leave a can of gasoline for you, and you can meet me at the sandbar in the morning, Everett. We can throw out an anchor line and kedge the runabout off the shoal." He winked at Grandpa. "I must say you made pretty good time in that canoe."

"I'm indebted to you, Jim," Grandpa called after Mr. Norkin. "I don't have to tell you how much we appreciate your help."

Mr. Norkin switched on his motor and waved his hand. "Glad to do it. Better keep that girl on a string." He laughed and steered his way out into the channel. I was sure he would go home and tell the story to Mrs. Norkin and Ned. I wondered what they would think. Did he know what I had done?

Grandma was leading Carrie up to the cottage, with Grandpa right behind them, like he wasn't letting Carrie out of his sight.

I followed them to the cottage. Halfway there Grandpa stopped and turned around to face me. "Don't be too hard on yourself, Mirabelle, but keep in mind Caroline is under our protection. We're all responsible for her. Her father trusts us to care for her. I'm not just talking about her physical welfare. If she'd been happy here, she'd never have done something so foolish and dangerous." He turned and stalked up the path, not holding the screen for me but letting it slam shut in my face. That was the worst moment of my life.

Grandma sent Tommy, Emily, and Nancy to bed and led Carrie upstairs to get out of her wet clothes.

I dragged up the stairway, thinking I'd spend the night on the sleeping porch. I didn't want to face Carrie, but Grandma found me there.

"Belle, you belong in your own room tonight with Carrie." She waited until I went into the room, closing the door behind me, shutting me in.

Carrie looked up. She was in a robe, drying her feet. She had a furious look on her face. I felt like Grandma had put me in a cage with a wildcat and locked the cage door.

"I suppose you're the one who told on me?"

I nodded.

"I hope you're satisfied." She threw the towel on the floor.

I stood there at the doorway, afraid of coming any farther into the room. "I should have kept you from going."

"It was none of your business."

I couldn't forget Grandpa's words. "We're responsible for you," I said.

She stared at me. "I don't want you to be responsible for me. I'm not some poor relation. I'm used to civilization, not to some godforsaken island in the middle of nowhere." She flung herself onto the bed and pulled the sheet over her head.

I didn't care what Grandma said. Carrie was wearing us all down like the water nudged the stones in the crib, loosening them one by one, until if you didn't rebuild the crib, everything was washed away.

Ten

When I awoke in the morning, the reflection of sun and water was dancing on the ceiling. For a second I looked forward to the summer day. Then I saw Carrie lying there, her blond hair spread out on the pillow, her mouth open a little. I remembered. What I had let happen to Carrie would be on everyone's mind. I decided to sneak out of the cottage and make my way to the storm side of the island without anyone seeing me.

I heard voices and then the sound of approaching boats. There would be no early-morning swim. Grandpa would be taking off with Mr. Norkin to recover the runabout. I went to the window, careful not to wake Carrie. There were two boats. Mr. Norkin was in his boat and Ned was in our canoe.

Grandpa was talking with Mr. Norkin, but he wasn't getting into Mr. Norkin's boat. I wondered why they weren't going after the runabout.

Grandpa grabbed one of the dock supports as if he needed to hang on to something. Mr. Norkin put a hand on Grandpa's shoulder, like you comfort a child. A minute later Ned climbed into Mr. Norkin's boat and they took off. Grandpa came up the path. He was bent over and walking slowly, as if he were carrying something heavy, but there was nothing in his hands.

I wondered if Grandpa was ill, if that was why he wasn't going to get the runabout. Maybe he and Mr. Norkin had been talking about the night before, and imagining what might have happened to Carrie had made Grandpa sick. Feeling worse than ever, I watched from the window until Ned and Mr. Norkin were out of sight.

I couldn't face Carrie. I reached for my shorts and a shirt that wasn't too wrinkled and took them into the bathroom to dress. Splashing water on my face didn't help. Neither did brushing my teeth or combing my hair. Everything seemed too much trouble, as if there were no point to it. Carrie was still asleep when I closed the bedroom door and started downstairs, wondering how I could sneak out of the cottage with no one seeing me.

Grandma and Grandpa were in the living room, their arms around each other. No one else was up. Grandma was crying. Grandpa's white hair was rumpled, and his glasses had slipped down his nose. He looked like that character in Shakespeare's play *King Lear*, who had his kingdom stolen right out from under him. I always imagined Lear shaking his fist at the heavens and wailing. Though he wasn't shaking his fist or wailing, that's what Grandpa looked like he wanted to do. It was all my fault. All I wanted was to disappear. I headed for the door, but Grandma saw me.

"Belle, come here, dear."

She didn't sound angry at me, only sad, which was worse.

I walked into the room, waiting for them to say something, prepared to be scolded. But no one mentioned the night before. Not then, or ever again.

"Something has happened, Belle," Grandma said. "Mr. Norkin brought us a telegram from the State Department." She waited as if she wanted someone else to finish what she was saying.

They were staring at me as if I didn't speak the same language they did and they were wondering how they were going to talk to me.

It was Grandpa who finally said, "Caroline's father has been killed in a bombing raid in England. It happened yesterday." He pushed up his glasses and smoothed his hair. "Caroline will have to be told."

It was the end of July and I felt like I was freezing. Up until that minute, war had been the newspaper headlines and reports on the radio. It was a nuisance that kept Mom and Dad in Detroit and Carrie on the island.

"Perhaps we should wait until Carrie's up and

dressed and had her breakfast," Grandma said.

Grandpa shook his head. "Look at us. She would know in a second something is wrong."

We heard Carrie open the bedroom door and start down the stairway. She had put on her robe and combed her hair. She came down the stairs, putting each foot down firmly. She looked at us, her chin up, her shoulders squared, ready to fight us. In a rush she said, "I want to leave here. I want to go back to Washington. I can stay with Louise until Papa comes back."

When she saw the way we were looking back at her, she lost her fight. Just as Grandpa had said, she saw that something was wrong.

Grandma put her arm around Carrie and led her to the davenport. "Sit down, dear. We have something to tell you."

Carrie looked at each one of us, waiting to see who would do the telling.

"We have sad news, Caroline," Grandpa said. "It's your father. There was a very bad air raid yesterday in London. We've had news that your father was caught in it. He didn't survive. I'm so sorry, my dear."

Carrie put her hands over her ears and ran out of the house, letting the screen door slam behind her.

Grandpa and Grandma looked at each other. Grandma started for the door.

"Wait," I said. "Let me go." Grandpa had said that we were all responsible for Carrie.

Grandpa studied me for a minute and then nodded. I walked out to the dock, where Carrie was sitting. I didn't have any words and Carrie didn't want any. I slipped down beside her and put my arm around her. We were both crying, but Carrie looked more angry than sad. Suddenly she threw off her robe and plunged into the water in her pajamas. She swam forty feet out into the channel. I was about to jump in after her when she stopped swimming out and began swimming parallel to the shore. I saw with amazement that there was no point in my going after her, as she was a much stronger swimmer than I was. Her arms shot in and out of the water. She hardly seemed to come up for air. I hadn't even known she could swim.

When she was nearly out of sight, she turned back. By now everyone was on the dock with me, watching. Polo's hackles were up. He must have thought the commotion out in the channel was some strange, wild animal. That's the way it looked.

Back and forth Carrie went, arms slicing the water, legs kicking up a froth. She must have swum more than a mile before she climbed out onto the dock, shaking off Grandpa's help. Water dripped from her pajamas. She tugged on her robe and marched into the cottage without a word, slamming the screen door behind her.

"Well, I'll be damned," Grandpa said, and he never swore.

"How come she's such a good swimmer?" Tommy asked.

"Maybe she's a mermaid," Nancy said.

Emily's eyes were huge. "I wonder what else she can do."

I had seen Carrie's defiant look as she passed me. I thought she could do anything.

It was after eleven when the rest of us had breakfast. Grandma had taken a tray up to Carrie, who refused to come down. Grandpa had gone over to the mainland to phone the State Department. When he returned, he went upstairs to talk with Carrie.

At the breakfast table Grandpa told the rest of us what he had told Carrie. Uncle Howard had been in London, walking to his apartment from the embassy. The people at the embassy guessed that when the air-raid sirens went off, he had only a short way to go and he kept walking instead of heading for the nearest shelter. A bomb had fallen, collapsing the building he was passing. In the fall the State Department would arrange a memorial service in Washington. We would all go with Carrie.

Nancy, who had tears in her eyes, asked, "What will happen to Carrie? She'll be an orphan."

"Please don't use that word, Nancy," Grandma said. "Of course Carrie must make her home with you."

Emily said, "We'll be her family now."

Grandpa said, "I phoned your mother and father.

They'll be calling Caroline to tell her how much they want her to live with them. She'll be better off with you children than with old people like us."

I realized Carrie would truly be my sister. What would that mean?

After breakfast I knocked on our bedroom door. I had never done that before, but now I was a little afraid of Carrie. Swimming out there, she had seemed so desperate.

Carrie flung open the door. "You don't have to knock. It's your room." Her eyes were red; her hair was pulled back into a fist of hair, thinning her face and giving her a skinned look. She wasn't wearing makeup, which made her look younger.

Her suitcase was open on her bed. "I don't want to stay here," she said. "I don't want to spend the rest of my life on an island in the middle of nowhere. Papa wouldn't have wanted me to."

She sank down on the chair, biting her lip to keep from crying. She was so miserable, I could hardly bear to look at her.

"We'll leave here the beginning of September, and then you'll live with us. You'll like Detroit. It's just like any city. We have movie houses and an art museum and dances at the high school every Friday when there's no basketball game." I was trying to think of things she would like.

"I won't know anyone. Everyone will be a stranger."

"You'll make friends. You're so pretty. Everyone will like you."

She looked at me. "You don't like me."

She surprised me into the truth. "I wanted to like you, but you wouldn't let me. You kept fighting us."

Carrie pulled her feet up under her. "You're such a closed circle. You're all so sanctimonious, so proud of your precious cottage, like it's the only place in the world."

"We do love it. You loved France. Why shouldn't people have places in the world they love?"

"It wasn't just France." Tears were streaming down her face. "It was all the things I did with Papa. He loved horse racing. He took me to the races at Longchamp and all the men wore top hats. Afterward we sat outside in a little café near the rose gardens and had ice cream. I rode with Papa on the bridle paths in the Bois. We went to Angélina on the rue de Rivoli on winter afternoons, where they have the best hot chocolate in the world. On the Fourth of July he took me to the American embassy for their garden party. He bought me a new hat to wear to the party."

I saw Carrie in riding breeches and a smart jacket on a bridle path, the scent of roses in the air. I saw her dressed in a frilly skirt, wearing white gloves and drinking hot chocolate, her father across from her, proud of how pretty she looked. I saw her in the garden of the embassy, holding a little plate of cookies and being introduced to important French people. I could see all those things clearly. I couldn't see her at the high school basketball game. I couldn't see her happily settled into the backseat of the car next June, nibbling chicken sandwiches, eagerly counting the miles until we reached the island.

"Even if you could pack up and go to Paris, it's full of German soldiers now," I said.

Carrie looked at me. "Don't be stupid. You still don't understand. It wasn't Paris. It was Papa."

Things happened very fast. Letters came from Mom and Dad trying to console Carrie, saying how much they looked forward to having Carrie with them, how she would be as much their child as we were. It was arranged that we would all go to the Lodge at a certain time so that Mom and Dad would be able to talk with Carrie by phone. Carrie listened to what they had to say, but she hardly said two words herself. It must have meant something, though, because when she was finished, she stood with the receiver in her hand looking around as if she were afraid to hang up, as if it might end the connection between her and my parents forever.

An official-looking letter of sympathy for Carrie came from the State Department, and another letter arrived for Grandpa about Uncle Howard's pension. There was an article in *The New York Times* about Uncle Howard's death with his picture. He had a pleasant face and a kind of amused smile, as if he knew he ought to look serious for the occasion but didn't care. A long letter came from Louise, who said she was very sorry about Uncle Howard's death. At the end of the letter she mentioned that she had a new job. It was that last letter that bothered Carrie the most. I think she had wanted to believe that if she could just go and live with Louise, somehow her father would reappear.

We all tried to cheer Carrie up and make her feel she was a part of our family. Carrie was determined not to be cheered and not to be a part of us. It was a kind of war. Not the kind in the newspapers, but the kind of siege you study in your history books, where one side is on top of a mountain and the other side on a field looking up at the mountain. One after another of us would try to climb the mountain, but Carrie kept fighting us off.

At first Grandpa said something about how we would all have to "carry on." "Work and routine will tide you over bumpy spots," he said. Grandpa had a lot of sayings like that. He added, "Well, Caroline, now that we all know what a fine swimmer you are, you'll have to join our early-morning dip."

I knew Carrie had no intention of doing that, and she didn't. Grandpa found other things to do. He organized a whole week of frantic activity, nearly killing all of us and getting nowhere with Carrie. He planned a picnic on the beach and used precious gasoline coupons for a boat ride to Mackinac Island with lunch at the elegant Grand Hotel. Two days were given over to painting the inside of the boathouse. He chopped down some dead trees for firewood and had us carry the wood and stack it into cords. By the end of the week all of us except Carrie were exhausted. Carrie hadn't exactly refused to go along with Grandpa's plans—she just hung back, dabbing with a paintbrush for a few minutes or carrying a hunk of wood or two and then wandering off. Even the trip to Mackinac Island was a failure.

"How many islands *are* there?" Carrie asked, as if we meant to torture her by dragging her to every island in the world when all she wanted was to find land where you weren't trapped inside a ring of water.

Like Grandpa, we all longed to do something for Carrie. Emily crept in and out of our bedroom, gathering up Carrie's wrinkled dresses to press and straightening up her drawers and dresser top. She spent her allowance on nail polish, files, and cuticle cream and begged to manicure Carrie's nails. At first Carrie seemed amused, but she soon grew impatient. Emily scorched one of her dresses and couldn't seem to get her nails filed evenly. The more impatient Carrie became, the harder Emily tried, until Grandma had to call Emily aside.

"Emily," Grandma said in a quiet voice, "right now Carrie needs a little time for herself."

Tommy was more successful. All summer he had

patiently been taming the chickadees that flocked to our bird feeder. He stood close to the feeder, sunflower seeds in his outstretched hands, trying to look like a bush or a small tree. At first the chickadees had made little darting pecks at the seeds, but after several days they had begun lighting on his hands and even his shoulders and head. It was so strange to see him, like a birdman. When he saw Carrie standing on the screen porch watching him, he called to her to come out. He made her stand just where he had stood and, giving her sunflower seeds, told her to hold out her hand. One by one the chickadees flew to her hand to take the sunflower seeds. At first she was startled by the light pecks as they snatched at the seeds, but after a few minutes she relaxed. A couple of times a day Carrie would go out and stand by the feeder and let the chickadees eat from her hand, but after a few days she shook her head when Tommy called to her.

Nancy was busy with her thousand things. Each morning she put out dried ears of corn for the deer. She was making bracelets for all of us for Christmas from the snail shells she found on the beach. The porch steps were covered with splatter paintings she did with leaves and a screen and toothbrush. She caught flies for a small toad she kept in an old glass fish tank she had filled with dirt and tiny plants. On hot afternoons Polo trotted along after her or sprawled by her side, his tongue lolling out. When she went to bed, Polo followed her up the stairs, his nails clicking against the wood, and disappeared into the sleeping porch, where he spent the night on the foot of Nancy's bed.

One evening Nancy appeared in our bedroom in her pajamas, Polo beside her. Carrie and I were both in bed with our lights out, but we were awake. That afternoon Nancy had been there when I had confided to Grandma, "Carrie isn't sleeping much. She tosses and turns, and sometimes I can hear her cry." I didn't tell Grandma that once when she'd been crying, I had gotten up and knelt down next to Carrie's bed and put an arm around her. Carrie had shaken off my arm and put her pillow over her head so I couldn't hear her.

"It's going to take time for Carrie," Grandma had said. "She just has to do her grieving."

When I saw Nancy standing there, I asked, "What's the matter? How come you're up?"

Nancy rubbed the sleep out of one eye. "Polo is really good at chasing away bad dreams," she said. "When he's sleeping on the foot of my bed, I never have a bad dream. I want to lend him to Carrie." She dragged Polo by the collar to Carrie's bed. She patted the bed, and Polo sprang up and settled at Carrie's feet. Nancy ordered, "Stay," and left the room, closing the door behind her.

Carrie looked at Polo, and for a minute I thought she was going to push him away like she had pushed me away. Instead, she reached down and scratched behind his ears. Then she lay down, Polo draped over her feet, and fell asleep. There was no crying that night.

Even Mrs. Norkin wanted to do something for Carrie. One evening before supper she sent everyone out of the kitchen and warned us all that we had to be in our seats right on time. We could hear her bustling back and forth and the sound of the eggbeater and the oven door opening and closing. When we'd finished the main course, she cleared the dinner plates herself, not allowing us to help and refusing to let us into the kitchen, even keeping Polo out.

"I don't want him stamping around," she said.

She disappeared into the kitchen, and after a wait while we all stared at one another, she marched into the dining room holding a dish with something chocolate showing up on the top.

"It's a soufflé," she said. "That's a French dessert." She set it down in front of Carrie. "You can dish out," she said.

Carrie looked up at Mrs. Norkin as if a caterpillar had turned into a butterfly right before her eyes. She grinned. It was the first smile since the day she had heard her father died.

Tommy stared at the soufflé. "A *hot* dessert?"

Carrie paid no attention to him but carefully dished out equal portions.

Mrs. Norkin stood by, not returning to the kitchen, waiting for Carrie to taste the soufflé.

"It's heavenly," Carrie said. "The best I've ever had." All the rest of us except Tommy, who was elaborately blowing on the dessert, chimed in.

That was a lot for Carrie to say. Most of the time she spoke only when she was spoken to. She hung on to every word as if she had only so many words and they had to last for the rest of her life. She and I often sat side by side saying nothing.

I didn't want to leave Carrie alone, so I had stopped going to the storm side of the island. Instead, on the hot August afternoons we would settle down on the dock and silently watch the gulls taking off and landing on Gull Rock. Sometimes we would walk the circle that was the island. We didn't even walk side by side but one behind the other, our bare feet sometimes on the hot sand and sometimes in the cool water. There were special places where without any words we both stopped for a few minutes. One place was a little stream that trickled into the lake, where each day we checked to see how large the tadpoles were getting to be. There was another place where horsetails grew. You could pull the tubes of grass apart and put them back together like a puzzle. For me it was just the useless, dumb activity that made summer so special. The serious way Carrie went at it made me think she was relieved to find something that could be pulled apart and put back together.

Sometimes Carrie would ask me about our house and our neighborhood and our school. Things had changed. Instead of the questions I had asked about Paris, Carrie was asking about the place that would be her new home. It must have seemed as exotic and distant to her as France seemed to me.

She said, "I've never had a backyard," and "I never learned to ride a bike." The question she asked most often was "What do you do?" as if she were trying to figure out how she was going to survive in some barren desert.

It was a scorching August day. We had on our bathing suits, but even so, I could feel sweat running down between my shoulder blades. The beach was too hot to walk on, and we splashed along on the scallops of wet sand. The air shimmered in the heat as if someone were shaking it. The water was as calm as a sheet of blue construction paper. Even the gulls seemed to drop down rather than land on Gull Rock, as if it were too much trouble to flap their wings. On some crazy impulse I stopped to pick up a gull feather and tucked it in Carrie's hair. She grinned at me. It was the same grin she had given the chocolate soufflé. "Race you to Gull Rock and back," she said.

She plunged into the water. I was right behind her, struggling to keep up. By the time I threw myself down beside her on the sand, I was panting.

"Where did you learn to swim?" I asked.

"Every August, to get away from the Paris heat, Papa and I used to go to Deauville on the northwest coast of France. It's right on the sea. Papa said if I was going to swim in the ocean, I had to be a good swimmer. He taught me. He would stand a little way out and I would swim to him. Then he stood farther out. That day when I heard he had died, I think I was swimming out to him. I wasn't sure I wanted to come back."

It was the first time since the day she'd heard of his death that she had mentioned her father. I didn't know what to say. Nothing must have been enough, for Carrie kept right on talking about her father.

"They have a famous racetrack there. We'd stay for the Grand Prix de Deauville. It was always held the fourth Sunday in August. Everyone got all dressed up. The men wore top hats. Papa looked so elegant in his morning coat." She was silent for a minute. "Remember that lilac organdy dress that Papa bought me at the Galeries Lafayette, the one I gave Emily? It was for the Grand Prix."

Carrie was actually talking with me as if I weren't the enemy.

"Sometimes Papa and I would go sailing." She gave me a sidewise glance. "How come Ned never comes by in his sailboat anymore?"

I couldn't say that he had been hurt by the way she had snubbed him, so I made an excuse. "I think he goes out fishing with his dad," I said. "With meat rationing people are eating a lot of fish. Mr. Norkin is sending most of his catch downstate."

Carrie was piling the warm sand on her legs and

feet. "He'd come by if you asked him to," she said.

Part of me thought it would be something I could do for Carrie, something to make up for her losing her father. Part of me didn't want to do it. Until Carrie had come, Ned had been my friend. The evenings we sailed together were the best part of the summer. I was never uncomfortable with him; we could tell each other anything. Now we were practically strangers and I was about to hand him over to Carrie. I thought it was like the night Nancy had lent Polo to Carrie. The comparison between Ned and Polo was funny, but I couldn't smile.

The next day Grandpa gave me letters to take to the mainland to mail and Grandma gave me a list of things to buy at the Norkins' vegetable stand. It was Mrs. Norkin's day to be at our cottage, so I knew I would find Ned minding the stand. I made some excuse and left without Carrie. I knew there would be no way I could ask Ned with Carrie standing next to me.

I found Ned sitting under the shade of an apple tree, the apples still small and green. He was reading a Detroit newspaper, which got to Birch Bay a day late. He grinned at me over the paper. "Our air force is giving the Germans a taste of their own medicine." He must have noticed I was thinking hard about something else. "What's the matter?" he asked.

I picked up one of the brown paper bags Mrs. Norkin saved from her grocery shopping and began filling it with pale-yellow butter beans. They were the skinny ones that you hardly had to cook.

"Come on, Belle, you're not worried about beans. What's up?"

"You never come by after dinner," I said, trying not to sound whiny.

He got up and started moving things around on the vegetable stand. Putting the broccoli where the cauliflower was and the cauliflower where the broccoli had been. "You guys are always busy," he said. After a minute he offered, "I could come by tonight and take you sailing."

I could have said yes, and Ned and I would have been back like we were, but I didn't. I had come for something else. "You could take Carrie out sailing."

Ned gave me a long look. "I don't think she's interested in coming sailing with me."

"She wants to go sailing with you. She asked why you didn't come around anymore."

"She's not stupid. She should know the answer to that. My dad told me all about what happened when she was trying to pick up Brad—"

"That's all over with," I cut in. "She's been really depressed since her father died."

"I'm sorry, but what am I supposed to do about it?" He smiled. "You've put enough beans in that bag to feed a hundred people."

I started pulling the beans out. "She's really unhappy, Ned. I think it would do her good to get away from the island with you for a couple of hours. Her dad used to take her sailing."

"So I'm supposed to be Papa?" he said. "Hey, you'll wear out the beans." He took the bag out of my hands and weighed the beans that were left. "Will you come along?"

I shook my head. "I think Carrie gets enough of me, enough of all of us, on the island."

"If you ask me, you're too good for her. I think the girl is confused. She could learn something from you and your family."

I was amazed. I had never occurred to me that Ned was thinking about our family, judging us. "I don't think Carrie sees it that way." I held out a dollar bill.

Ned handed me the change. "Like I said, she's confused."

Twelve

Grandma had long since turned the calendar in the kitchen from July's picture of a cornfield to August's picture of farmers in a field cutting wheat. On the mainland the hard red blackberries were a ripe, soft purple. Mrs. Norkin brought us quarts and quarts of berries to sprinkle over our cereal and bake into pies. Birdsong disappeared. The silence in the trees was as quick as lifting a needle from a phonograph record.

"They don't sing much after the baby birds have flown," Tommy explained. "The birds aren't territorial anymore." He grinned, proud of using a big word.

Mom and Dad sent Carrie pictures of our house and the front and back yards. "So you'll know where you'll be living," Mom wrote Carrie. "We are looking forward to having you with us." The pictures were so familiar to me, it was hard to believe they were new to Carrie. I looked to see what she would see. Would she notice the path into the backyard tangle of shrubbery where Nancy put out lettuce for the rabbits or the bird feeder Tommy had made from a tomato can? Dad had taken a picture of the whole family by setting the camera and then running to stand beside us. You could see he looked more hurried than the rest of us. Was Carrie trying to imagine herself in the picture?

She glanced at the snapshots and tossed them onto the dresser as if they were postcards of a country she had no interest in visiting.

After I talked with him, Ned came by the next night. Carrie hurried out to meet him, never bothering to ask if I wanted to come sailing with them. I stood on the dock and watched Ned's sailboat skimming over the water, surprised at how lonely I felt with my whole family around me. I wondered if that was how Carrie felt, lonely with all of us around her.

The next night, although Carrie stood out on the dock waiting, Ned didn't show up. He didn't appear the night after that either. When I asked Carrie if she wanted to go over to the mainland with me to do some errands, she shook her head.

"No point. It's too depressing. There's nothing there."

I was sure something had happened, and later when I saw Ned going into the hardware store, I waited for him. He was inside a long time, long enough for me to decide to leave and then to change my mind a hundred times. He frowned when he saw me.

"What are you doing here? You've caused me enough trouble!"

"I was waiting for you, and what do you mean, caused you trouble?"

Ned looked around him. "Come on over here." He led me toward a park bench the city fathers had set up in memory of something or other.

"Do you know what that crazy cousin of yours wanted me to do?"

"Carrie?" I just looked at him, my mouth open. I couldn't guess what he was going to say, but I was sure I wouldn't like it.

"Yes, Carrie. She wanted me to elope with her. She said we should get married and go to New York or Washington to live. She said she could get some money from her father's estate. I'm only seventeen and she's only fifteen. She said we could lie about our ages. No one would believe her, and even if they did, I'd end up behind bars instead of in the Navy."

I believed every word he said. It sounded just like Carrie. I was so angry, I could have slapped her. We had done everything we could for her. I had even given her Ned, and she'd hatched a wild scheme that would have gotten Ned into trouble. "Does your mother know?" I asked.

"Do you think I'm out of my head? My folks would have a fit. You're the only one I've told, and don't you tell anyone. Now I've got to get back. Dad's waiting for some bolts." He suddenly smiled at me. "If you want to go out sailing, let me know, but I'm keeping clear of your crazy cousin."

On the way back I tried to think what to do. Summer was coming to an end. In a couple of weeks I'd be back in the city wearing shoes and doing homework. Not only would we have to go back home, but this year we would take Carrie with us. We were stuck with her forever. If it had been anyone except Ned, I would have loved to see her elope and run off to New York.

I found Carrie in our room. She looked at me. "Ned told you, didn't he? It's written all over your face. You can save the lecture. I don't care."

I was furious. "You don't care about anything. You certainly don't care about Ned. You would have let him ruin his whole life just so you could get away from here. Why? We've gone out of our way to do everything we could think of for you."

Carrie flung the magazine she had been reading onto the floor. "That's not what I want. I don't want to be fussed over like a sick animal that has to be humored and cheered up. Everybody treats me like some bizarre creature who's dropped out of the sky. You won't let me be a member of your family unless I turn into one of you, and I'd rather die."

I ran out of the room. I couldn't go downstairs. My face was streaked with tears. I didn't want anyone to see me. Grandpa and Grandma were in the living room, Tommy and Emily in the yard. I turned and stumbled up the stairs to the attic. I heard our bedroom door open. Carrie followed me up the stairs.

I didn't want to see her. I didn't want to see anyone. I wanted to figure things out. Something Carrie said had stung. Maybe it was true. Maybe we had tried too hard to make her be like us. I wondered if the island kept things out as well as keeping things in.

Carrie was at the top of the attic stairway. "I'm sorry," she said. "I didn't mean to scream at you." She was crying, too. "I guess I thought if I could run away, I could run away from what happened to Papa. I just didn't want to think about it anymore. I didn't mean to get Ned in trouble. Even if he had agreed, and I guess I knew he wouldn't, I probably would never have done it." She looked nervously around the attic. "What's all this stuff?"

I felt my anger at Carrie petering out. I sighed and looked at the neatly labeled trunks and boxes that covered the attic floor. "Grandma and Grandpa never throw anything away."

Carrie wandered around scanning the labels. She stopped at one of the trunks. "This trunk has my mother's name on it," Carrie said. "What's it doing *here*?"

"Your mother spent all her summers on the island until she married your father."

She seemed stunned.

"Do you want to open it?"

Carrie stood staring down at the trunk. "Papa never kept any of my mother's things," she said. "I think he was so upset when she died, he couldn't bear to have anything of hers around. There was just her picture that he took wherever we went and a ring and some pearls he was saving for me." She looked wary, as if she were afraid of what was inside the trunk. "You open it," she said.

I had to fuss with the trunk's catches to get them to work. When it was open, Carrie stood looking at it, a worried expression on her face, as if touching the trunk might cause it to disappear. After a minute she lifted out a dress. It was a typical twenties dress with a dropped waistline, a pleated skirt, and a sailor collar. Holding it up to herself, she looked at me, surprised and smiling. "It's just my size. Do you think Grandma would let me have it?"

"Sure. It's *your* mom. All those things probably belong to you."

She began pulling out more dresses, mostly summer cottons but one party dress of pale-blue chiffon. There was an autograph book, each page scrawled with verses and messages. When a dried rose pressed between two pages shattered into pieces, Carrie looked devastated. She hastily put the book down. Beside it was a sketchbook. After what had happened with the rose, Carrie just looked at it, afraid to open it, but I was curious.

"What is it?" I asked.

Carrie lifted it carefully from the trunk. I peered over her shoulder. The words "My Island Garden" were neatly lettered on the cover, the letters decorated with twining ivy. On the first page was a watercolor of a garden with hundreds of tiny flowers and the cottage in the background.

"It's the garden out front," Carrie said. Despite what I'd just said, I think it was the first time she really connected her mother with the island. I doubt it had ever occurred to her that her mother had spent her summers here just as we did.

The picture of the garden was divided into sections, and each section was labeled with the name of a flower. When Carrie turned the pages, you could see watercolors of the flowers, mostly wildflowers. The watercolors were delicately colored and showed the flowers and their leaves. Brightly colored butterflies hovered over the blossoms. "There were lots more flowers in the garden then than there are now," Carrie said. She studied one of the pages. "Dutchman's-breeches. What an odd name."

"The flowers look like the trousers Dutchmen used to wear."

"Look," Carrie said. "Lavender. Just like I planted. It's almost like my mother was telling me what to plant." She gathered up her mother's dresses and the sketchbook and ran down the stairs. I was right behind her, curious about what she was going to do.

Clutching everything to her, she rushed into the

living room and confronted Grandma. "Can I have these?" she asked. "They're my mother's."

Startled, Grandma looked from Carrie to the dresses and sketchbook. "Why, of course. If I had only thought, I would have given them to you long ago. But what will you do with them, dear?"

"I'll wear the dresses, and I want to make the garden just like it was when my mother had it."

Grandma frowned. "Those dresses are a little out of fashion, I'm afraid."

"They're just Carrie's size," I pleaded.

Grandma understood. "I think they would be fun to wear, Carrie. Just on the island, of course."

Grandpa shook his head. "Restoring the garden would take a lot of hard work, Caroline. You'd never get it done in the couple of weeks we have left."

Carrie's eyes sent blue sparks in Grandpa's direction. I knew she meant to have her way. There were waves of energy around her, as if any minute she would fly off in several directions. Grandpa must have felt it, too.

"Well, no harm in trying, I guess." He buried his head in the newspaper. Carrie swept up the stairway. We could hear closet doors banging.

"She must be hanging those old clothes up," Grandma said. "I can't think what she wants with them. They're from a different age."

I thought I knew. In all the years since her mother had died, her arms around those dresses was as close as Carrie had come to her.

All afternoon Carrie studied her mother's garden book. After dinner she hunted up a spade, marched out to the garden, and began digging.

"Grandma," Emily wailed, "Carrie's digging up my marigolds." Planting lavender in the garden was one thing, digging up marigolds another.

From the window we could see Carrie plunging the spade into the soil as if she were after buried treasure, as if hunks of gold were just under the surface and would disappear if she didn't hurry. The marigolds flew every which way.

Grandma said, "Your aunt Julia never had marigolds in her garden, Emily."

"But they're blooming." Emily was ready to run outside.

Grandma put a hand on her shoulder. "Let her be, dear. It's the first time I've seen Carrie actually interested in something."

By the time Carrie had finished, it was almost dark. It had been like watching her swimming. She had so much energy, she could have lighted up a whole city. Grandpa trundled out the wheelbarrow and helped Carrie load it with garden discards and clumps of grass that had overgrown the garden.

When I got ready for bed, Carrie was still poring over the sketchbook. "Grandma says most of these flowers are wildflowers and that they grow in the woods. How am I supposed to find them?"

Leafing through the book, I recognized several of the flowers Aunt Julia had painted. "I know where some of them are. Emily and Nancy and Tommy can help. That one I'm sure just grows on the mainland. We'd have to hunt over there."

"Will you help me?" Carrie asked.

Carrie had never asked me for anything, and everything I had given without her asking hadn't worked out. I wanted to shrug off what she was asking, to tell her that a lot of wildflowers nearly disappeared after they bloomed, that I didn't care that much for wildflowers anyhow. I think it's a good thing that sometimes when you are rushed into something, you make the right decision even if you don't want to. I think it means that inside people there's a lot of good stuff just waiting to pop out. Anyhow, before I could say no, I said, "Yes."

Thirteen

The mulleins were easy. Their yellow flowers and gray lambswool leaves stuck up in spires, some of them as tall as Nancy. Carrie wanted to dig up the tall ones, but when Grandpa saw what she was doing, he said, "Take the smallest ones. They'll be most likely to survive."

Carrie took the tallest ones. Digging them up killed their long roots, and by the second day they were dead. She went back and dug up the little ones.

"Well, the child's capable of learning," Grandpa mumbled.

The wild asters were just beginning to bloom, pink ones and white ones and purple ones with yellow centers. Carrie put them in the place that Aunt Julia had marked out for them.

"How do all these flowers get onto the island?" Carrie asked.

"Bird poop," Tommy said. "The birds eat the

flower seeds and then drop them on the island."

Tommy discovered a large patch of trout lilies. They didn't look like much, but in the spring the plants would be covered with small yellow blossoms.

Nancy, who loved picking berries, led us to a patch of wild strawberries. We had consulted the book and found that Aunt Julia had edged the garden with the tiny plants that would bloom early in the spring and have clusters of small red berries toward the end of June. We filled in a patch of Dutchman's-breeches and another patch with evening primrose. None of us kids had known that the tall yellow flowers that bloomed in the late afternoon had a name.

"When I was a girl," Grandma said, "we used to call them four-o'clocks because that's when the flowers started to open up."

Everyone got involved. Grandpa found the Saint-John's-wort. We hadn't remembered it although we must have passed it a million times. Grandpa brought out his magnifying glass and showed us how all the petals had rows of translucent dots along the edges like a row of little windows.

"Why wort? Why such an ugly name?" Carrie asked.

Grandpa always liked being asked questions because he usually knew the answer. He said, "Wort, not wart. Wort is an old English word for root or plant."

It was Grandpa who took us to the mainland to

find two blue plants we couldn't find on the island, chicory and viper's bugloss. The chicory grew along the roadside and had a root a yard long. After we searched a half dozen fields, it was Nancy who spotted the viper's bugloss.

That day in the fields on the mainland we found wild tiger lilies, and Queen Anne's lace with its carroty smell and frothy flowers, and a patch of butter-and-eggs that still had a few bright yellow blooms. Carrie laughed at the name, but it was right there neatly printed out in Aunt Julia's book.

Even Mrs. Norkin had something to give Carrie. For years she had raised lady's slippers from seeds. When she heard Carrie was looking for lady's slippers, she said, "You'd hardly notice them when they're not blooming, Carrie. I'll bring you some next time I come. They're scarce, so I don't dig up the plants. I gather the seeds and plant them." She was as good as her word. Two days later she appeared with four healthy plants all potted up in Campbell's soup cans.

Carrie beamed at Mrs. Norkin. The soup cans might have been filled with jewels.

I hardly knew this Carrie. She plunged into the garden the way she had plunged into the water the day she learned her father had died. She was still bossy, still insisting on being in control. She was stubborn. She never let us forget it was her garden. She never gave up on a flower, even if the flowers she transplanted died, like the mulleins had, and she had to plant them all over again. She was so set on copying her mother's garden that she was willing to do anything, just as she had been ready to run off with Ned to get away from the island. She was determined to make the garden exactly like her mother's, and she needed us to do it. We weren't the enemy anymore. We were on her side.

I had seen some of the flowers she was looking for on the storm side of the island. Carrie followed me carrying a pail and a trowel. We found tall spikes of purple loosestrife along the little steam that trickled into the lake. I pointed out tiny pale-pink flowers and their pointed seed pods that Aunt Julia had called cranesbill. We found a whole patch of them, still blooming, along the edge of the sand. Best of all were the wild roses that grew right in the sand. When Carrie saw them, her eyes got huge. She sniffed their fragrance and, ordering me to help her, carefully dug up the smallest shoots that would have the best chance of being transplanted.

"In a couple of years they'll have as many blooms as these bushes do," Carrie said. "We'll have enough roses to cut and bring inside."

Carrie went on digging but I stopped. I was thinking about what she had said. "In a couple of years . . . *we'll* have." Of course I knew that Carrie was going to live with us, and I knew we would come back to the island next year, but Carrie had fought so hard against being on the island, and now she was actually talking about what would happen when she returned.

My silence alerted Carrie. She looked up at me and, seeing the smile on my face, must have guessed what I was thinking. "For anyone who's here, that is."

Tommy came upon a patch of violets, the one flower missing from the garden. They were long past blooming, and the tiny heart-shaped leaves were hard to see in the grass. Carrie planted the violets in the part of the garden where a nearby maple tree would give them shade in the summer. She had found an old garden book of Grandma's and read about each flower she planted: which ones needed sun and which ones needed shade, the ones that did best in sandy soil and the ones that needed moist soil. When we had gone several days without rain, Carrie lugged pails of water the hundred-foot stretch from the lake, tipping the water into the sprinkling can.

After Grandpa noticed Carrie bent over to one side as she carried the heavy pail, he went to the mainland and bought a second pump to connect to the pipe that brought our water in from the lake, rigging up a faucet right next to the garden. Carrie watched all afternoon as Grandpa worked. When he was finished, Carrie put her arms around Grandpa and gave him a hug, surprising his glasses right off his nose.

Grandpa flushed. "I should have done it long ago. This way you can all rinse your feet after you come up from the beach."

Nancy sat down next to Polo every morning to explain that the garden was off limits. I didn't know whether he understood her or he remembered the scolding Carrie had given him when he had trampled the wild asters, but he obeyed.

Emily had forgiven Carrie the marigolds. "The garden will be so pretty next spring." She sighed. "Like the one in the book." Emily was reading *The Secret Garden*.

Grandma said, "What a lovely garden you have created, Carrie."

Carrie seemed surprised and then pleased. Later she said to me, "I can't believe I actually did something right." She grinned. "The garden will be my part of the island." She stood there looking down at the garden, which was mostly green now. I was sure she was seeing it as it would be in spring, with the lady's slippers and violets and trout lilies all in bloom. The amazing thing was she looked like she wanted to be here in the spring to see it. I thought all winter long she would be thinking of the island, just like I would, and just like me she would be eager to get back here.

Fourteen

While we were all busy helping Carrie with the garden, the August days had grown shorter. There were cool days when you had to pull on a sweater, the rough wool strangely scratchy against your skin. The fishing fell off—only sunfish and perch. The trees lost their fresh green and got a dusty look. Much to Tommy's sorrow the summer birds began to fly south; blackbirds flocked and the gulls were restless, swooping down on Gull Rock and then taking off again. We didn't want to, but little by little we began to think about returning home. It was like opening a book you had read before.

On a hot afternoon when not a leaf fluttered and Polo was so warm he watched a squirrel get within a foot of him and never moved a muscle, Grandpa said, "Mirabelle, why don't you take Caroline out and get her up to speed on the runabout."

Carrie and I both looked at him and then at each

other, amazed. It was as if Carrie's accident with the runabout had never happened. Grandpa didn't miss the look. "Well, it makes sense. Caroline is going to be here every summer."

Carrie already knew the basics, so I pointed out all the red buoys and where the shoals were and we practiced docking the runabout. Out on the water together, away from the island, Carrie seemed different, less sure of herself. "I suppose everyone at your school will think I'm weird and hate me."

"Carrie, that's crazy! You'll have the boys falling all over you."

"What about the girls? What about friends?"

I was going to say that it would be easy for her to make friends with the girls, but I wasn't sure, so I didn't get the words out fast enough.

"You don't think they'll like me."

"It's just that you come on so strong. You don't give people a chance to know you—you tell them what they ought to know."

I waited for Carrie to be angry. Instead she said, "I know that. When I was living with Papa, I was always with adults. I think Papa encouraged me to show off to his friends. He thought it was cute. This summer was the first time I was so close to someone my own age. You guys should have come with directions." She grinned at me. "But we're friends, *n'est-ce pas?*"

"We're friends, but go easy on the French."

"*Mais oui*." She took the wheel of the runabout and brought it expertly into the boathouse.

That evening I saw Ned sailing a little distance out from the cottage as if he wanted to be sure I was by myself. When he could see Carrie wasn't there, he sailed in and picked me up. I had forgotten how quiet a sailboat was. You didn't hear the roar of a motorboat, just the quiet lap of the water and the wind that was only a whisper.

"You don't have to be afraid of Carrie anymore," I told Ned.

He bristled. "I'm not afraid of her. I'm just not interested in being a part of her wild schemes. Mom says she's all wrapped up in some garden."

"It's so strange, Ned, how important the garden is to her. She didn't care anything about the island until she discovered what her mother did here. She even wears her mother's old dresses. I know she loved her father, but I don't think she knew that much about her mother. Now that she's discovered how her mother felt about the island, it's changed how she feels about it."

Ned didn't want to talk about Carrie. He was caught up in his own plans to join the Navy in the spring. I worried about Ned being in the middle of the ocean—an ocean would be very different from the channel—but he was so excited, I kept my worries to myself. Next summer, I thought, when we come, Ned won't be here. I hadn't wanted things to change on the island. First Carrie had come and now Ned was leaving.

"If you join the Navy, how long will you be gone?"

"Depends on the war. One year, two years."

A lifetime. "And then will you come back?" I wanted a time when I could think of being with Ned again.

"There's some talk of giving anyone who has served in the armed forces tuition for college. If that happens, I'll take it. Mom and Dad can't afford to send me. With fewer tourists Dad isn't guiding anymore, and Mom isn't selling a lot from her stand."

"After college you'd come back?"

"Probably not."

"Why not? It's perfect here," I insisted.

"It's perfect for you because you're just here in the summer, doing nothing. It's different if you live here and have to work all summer to make a living. I'm not crazy about fishing like Dad. I don't see any future for me up here. You ought to try one of our winters. It starts snowing in October and it's still snowing in May. You should see this town in January. It's one big snowdrift, with everyone sitting around twiddling their thumbs waiting for you summer people to come so we can work again."

I was devastated. I didn't know what was more crushing, thinking that I might never see Ned again or having him refer to me as "you summer people."

He must have seen the hurt on my face. "I'm not saying there's anything wrong with summer people. Mom and Dad think of your folks as family. It's just that I want to see more of the world. I haven't even been to Detroit, and I promise when I get there, I'll look you up. Anyhow, that's enough about me. What about you?"

"We'll be back, only this time Carrie will come with us." I sighed. "I'm not sure how that'll work out."

"Your mom and dad'll have their hands full."

"Carrie's changed. She's more a part of the family here, but I'm not sure how she'll fit in at home."

"Look, that's her problem. Let her be Carrie. Why are you worrying about it?"

"She's so different."

"You're all different. Your kid brother and your sisters are all characters. Mom says each one of you has a unique personality. You don't notice because you're used to each other. You'll get used to Carrie, too." Laughing, he splashed water on me. "So will you show me around Detroit when I visit you?"

Darkness was coming earlier. Ned and I tried to see the green flash that came just before the sun set into the water. Dad had explained the flash's scientific meaning, but I liked to think that, like a rainbow, it was a promise of another summer's day. As the boat skimmed over the water and the gulls hovered and plunged, Ned and I talked about what the future would be like. I sighed, because I knew whatever it would be like, it would never again be like this.

It was the Thursday before Labor Day. None of us wanted to think about the holiday weekend and how it would mean returning home. We were pretending the summer would go on forever. Except for Carrie we were all on the porch. Grandpa was reading the newspaper. "Those Danes are brave people," he said. "They're refusing to collaborate with the Germans."

As I listened to Grandpa, I was thinking that next year at this time Ned might be on a warship and in the middle of a battle. Half of Grandma's attention was on what Grandpa was saying and half on the beans she was stringing for supper. Emily was painting her toenails with Carrie's polish, hoping Grandma was too busy to notice. Tommy had his binoculars trained on a hawk perched on the top of a pine tree. Nancy, sprawled on the floor, was brushing Polo's coat, promising him she would visit him back in the city at Grandma and Grandpa's. Ned was right. We were all different from one another.

Carrie walked through the porch. I thought she meant to do some last thing in the garden. Instead, without a word she headed for the dock. A minute later she was unhitching the lines to the runabout, turning on the blower, switching on the ignition.

Grandpa stood up, the newspapers sifting down

from his lap to make a little pile on the porch floor. I waited for him to call to Carrie, to tell her to stop, but he just stood there watching her carefully ease the runabout out into the channel. I thought I saw her wave, but it all happened so fast, I couldn't be sure. I knew what she was doing. Grandpa had said she should learn how to use the runabout. She was showing him that not only had she learned, she had learned well.

Grandpa marched down the path to the dock with all of us like a string of ducklings right behind him. We stood there, hypnotized, as Carrie disappeared around a bend.

"Maybe she won't come back," Tommy said.

"Shame on you, Tommy," Grandma scolded. She had a worried look on her face.

"She'll be back," Grandpa said. He headed for the porch.

In fifteen minutes Carrie was back. She docked the boat without effort and secured the lines. When she reached the porch, Grandpa was reading the newspaper. He didn't look up.

Grandma said, "We're having iced raspberry juice, Carrie. Will you have some?"

"Yes, please," Carrie said. She looked at Grandpa; Grandpa put the paper down and looked right back. Carrie's look said she would be one of the family but she would still be Carrie. Grandpa's look said, "Yes, but it's my decision to let you be Carrie."

I realized with a shock that Grandpa didn't mind

a little independence, that you could be independent and he'd still be there watching over you to see that you were safe. Carrie had opened a door for me. I saw that like the stone cribs, Grandpa and the rest of the family supported us, holding us together, but like the stones in the cribs, each one of us was different from the others and that was all right.

That same day a letter came for Carrie from Mom. She sent Carrie pictures of the room she was fixing up for Carrie. I found Carrie out on the porch studying the snapshots. She was frowning, and I thought something about the decoration was making her unhappy.

Carrie gave me a reproachful look. "There's only one bed in this room. I suppose you told your parents you didn't want to room with me."

I felt my cheeks burn. Mom had written to ask if I thought Carrie would like to share my bedroom or have a room of her own. Thinking of the mess that was our room in the cottage, I had written back that Carrie would probably like her own room. What I really meant was that I wanted my own room. But it wasn't just selfishness; I honestly believed that Carrie would be happy to be rid of me.

I managed to get out, "I thought maybe you wouldn't want to room with me."

"I never said that," Carrie answered.

"I'll write to Mom. I'll tell her we want to be together."

"That would be *très intime*." Carrie grinned.

"Carrie was disappointed not to be sharing a room with me," I wrote to Mom. Then I added, "We like being together." Amazingly, I decided it was true. We had grown together like the tangle of lavender plants that had made a hedge in Carrie's garden.

Labor Day weekend we closed up the cottage. It was a routine we went though each year. We packed our clothes, stored any food in tins so the mice wouldn't get to it, stripped the beds, and threw sheets over the upholstered chairs and davenport. Grandpa dragged the canoe up from the beach and with Mr. Norkin's help hoisted the runabout and the Chris-Craft in the boathouse. Grandpa cleaned the ashes out of the fireplace, drained the water pipes, and put up the shutters, shutting the eyes of one room after another.

I thought Carrie would be eager to get away, but instead she seemed uneasy about leaving. Her suitcases were strewn all over the bedroom, so we were always stumbling over them, but nothing seemed to get packed. Carrie spent her time curled up on the porch studying gardening books.

"It says to mulch your garden," she said. "What does that mean?"

"In a city garden," Grandma explained, "you would put down a layer of straw, but if you do that here, the mice will make their nests in the straw and nibble all the plants. Just let nature's mulch do the work. The leaves from the maple tree and the pine needles will settle over the garden."

At lunch Carrie said, "September might be dry." She had a worried look on her face, as if the whole world might burn up. "Some of the flowers were transplanted just last week. They'll need water."

Mrs. Norkin, who had come over that day to help close the cottage, said, "Ned will be out sailing. I'll have him stop by every couple of days and give them a watering."

Carrie blushed. "He probably wouldn't want to." I knew she was thinking about his reaction when she'd asked him to run away. She was sure he didn't want to have anything more to do with her.

"He'll do it if I ask him. He'd better." Mrs. Norkin patted Carrie's shoulder. "That garden's going to be just fine. Next year with Ned gone, you can come over and give me a hand with my garden."

We couldn't all fit into one car, so Tommy, Nancy, and Emily, along with Polo, would be driving back with Grandma and Grandpa. Carrie and I would go back in the bus. A couple of months ago I would have hated the idea of the long ride with Carrie, but now I was looking forward to showing her all the landmarks we watched for. When we returned next year, it would all be familiar to her. Carrie and I had been two islands. Little by little we had moved into each other's worlds until it was hard to tell where one began and the other ended.

There was time for one quick visit to the storm side of the island. Carrie was busy with her garden, so I went by myself. The leaves of the birch trees were turning yellow. Lake Huron nudged the sand, pulling it away from the island and washing it back. The restless gulls flew inland and then sailed back over the water as if they were rehearsing for the day they would leave. I realized it had been weeks since I had come here to dream of adventure in distant places. I hadn't needed to. The summer had been full of unexpected things happening. We had spent three months away from Mom and Dad. Ned was going off to war. Uncle Howard had been killed. But Carrie had been the real adventure. She had brought out the worst in us and the best in us.

I knew there would be problems when we got home. Carrie would have to get used to Mom and Dad and they would have to get used to her. It was hard to imagine her in our school, walking home with the kids, going to basketball games. But then I hadn't been able to imagine her before she came to the island. That's what had been so exciting about the summer. My books were exciting, but they ended. Carrie wouldn't end. With Carrie you would never know. She would go on changing us and we would go on changing her, but our war was over.

Gloria Whelan

is the bestselling author of many novels for young readers, including *Homeless Bird*, winner of the National Book Award, and *Listening for Lions*. She lives in northern Michigan. You can visit her online at www.gloriawhelan.com.